Merry MAYHEM

NEW YORK TIMES BESTSELLING AUTHOR

ERIN NICHOLAS

ABOUT THE BOOK...

In Rebel, Louisiana, Christmas isn't a holiday—it's a full-contact sport.

As a firefighter, I thought I'd seen holiday chaos before—fires caused by too many string lights, a Santa stuck in a chimney, one unfortunate incident with a candy cane—but this small town takes Christmas to a whole new level.

It all starts when I'm asked to pose as a fake boyfriend for the town's annual holiday competition. Easy gig: play games, drink cocoa, smile big, take home the trophy.

But my "date's" plans go sideways—literally—and while she's in the hospital, I'm left to handle all the plastic candy canes, Grinch impersonators, and deconstructed gingerbread houses with her sister instead. Single mom Thea is the calm, practical one who wants nothing to do with small-town drama... or me.

Too bad sparks fly anyway. Between her no-nonsense attitude, that soft heart she tries to hide, and the way she looks at me in the dark hallway when everyone else is asleep? It's not the tree at risk of going up in flames. Because *this* feels real and now I know exactly what I'm asking Santa for this year.

Christmas in Rebel isn't just *Merry*—it's absolute *Mayhem*.

CONTENT WARNING

Merry Mayhem is a very light, small town rom com with holiday hijinks, laugh-out-loud moments, and steamy scenes!

But, there are a few topics that are a little heavier and I want you to be aware.

The following things occur in the story:
- Automobile Accident / Injury (off-page, referenced)
- Medical Trauma / Stroke (off-page, referenced)
- Concussion / Medically-Induced Coma

The hero also starts out <u>fake</u> dating one sister and falling in love with the other, but there is *no* cheating or love triangle in this book, I promise!

If any of the above is going to cause you any trouble at all, please close the book now and return it. I want my books to bring nothing but good feelings!

If you read on, I hope you enjoy Merry Mayhem, the town of Rebel, Louisiana, and Josh and Thea's story!

xo Erin

CHAPTER 1
THEA

"ARE you *sure* you don't want me to take your shift tonight?" I ask my sister for the second time.

Violet shakes her head. "No. I'm fine. No big deal. I knew he'd be home for the holidays."

Yes, of course, her ex is home for Christmas. His parents, grandparents, and two sisters live here.

"But Ashley's with him," I say.

I'd seen Scumbag Sam and his new girlfriend earlier at the grocery store. I'd been chatting with Brian Watkins about his elbow surgery, so I couldn't flip Sam off, or turn my back on him, or even duck behind the display of pie filling to avoid him. Unfortunately, as the physical therapist in town—a healthcare provider and business owner—I have to act professionally and maturely, at least in public.

So, when Sam said, "Hey, Thea," I had to smile and say, "Hi, Sam." I had to be friendly and pleasant to the asshole who had broken my sister's heart. The same asshole who made her quit the job where they'd worked together, and move out of the apartment they'd shared, which is why, ten months later, she's still back home, working for our grandpa.

"I figured he would be," Violet says. "But I'm fine to work. Everything is fine."

I look around Perks and Rec, our grandfather's coffee shop/bar/café. It's busy right now due to the dinner rush, which will keep her distracted, but it will clear out quickly after everyone has eaten.

Merry Mayhem, the town's annual Christmas celebration, starts the day after tomorrow, and people will head home to get ready.

Yes, Merry Mayhem requires days of preparation. Weeks, even. And not just by the town's Parks and Recreation department, which is solely responsible for the various events and decorations around town, but for *everyone*. Because everyone in town participates. Everyone.

And then they'll all do it again for Valentine's Day. And then for St. Patrick's Day. And then…

I love my hometown.

I really do.

But it's exhausting at times.

Like now.

Not only is Merry Mayhem only a couple of days away, but my sister is having a personal crisis in the middle of it—actually *because* of it—and I just really want to put on pajamas, pop some popcorn, and put in a *funny* Christmas movie. Nothing with tears. Nothing like *The Family Stone*. I love that freaking movie, but I don't want to cry. I'm too tired to cry. I want to laugh. We're talking *Christmas Vacation* or *Elf* here.

But I won't. At least not until I know for sure Violet is okay.

"Okay, what can we do?" I ask, looking from Violet, who is bartending and waiting tables, to my cousin, Nora, and best friend, Anderson.

Nora is practically bouncing on her stool. Getting her to sit still this long is a miracle, honestly. It's a testament to how much she loves Violet. Nora is the head of Parks and Rec, and Merry Mayhem not only falls under her purview but also her invention.

She is dying to wrap something in twinkle lights or stick more paper snowflakes somewhere. Though I can't imagine she's missed a single surface.

Anderson is the one I should focus on. She's the most likely of us to come up with a way to really torture Violet's ex *and* to make it look like an accident. Or, better yet, make it look like his new girlfriend's fault. Andi has a mean streak, but only when it comes to men and *almost* only when it comes to scumbag men.

"Nothing," Violet says, waving her hand as if brushing a fly away. "It's fine."

That's the fourth 'fine' I've gotten.

"Violet," Nora says gently, taking Violet's hand. "Sam told me they're signing up for Merry Mayhem." She says it carefully, as if preparing for Violet to freak out.

That's exactly what we're expecting.

Violet does take a deep breath, but then she nods. "I expected that, too."

"You did?" I frown and look at Nora, then Andi.

"You're shocked?" Andi asks me.

Sam and Violet were together for *four years*. I thought I knew him well, too. "I honestly didn't think he'd be a big enough asshole to sign up for Mayhem without Violet the *first* year he's back."

Merry Mayhem is only in its fifth year this year. Sam and Violet did Merry Mayhem together every single year, and they won every time. Basically, there has never been a Merry Mayhem without Sam and Violet. Or a Sam and Violet without Merry Mayhem.

They displayed those stupid trophies on the bookcase in their living room in the apartment they shared until February this year. I don't know if they split them up when Violet moved out, or if she took all four, or if she threw them at him when he broke things off, or what, but those damned things were important to them at one time.

"You're doing so great," Andi tells Violet. "So, what if he

competes with someone new, right? You're going to show him that you don't care. That you've moved on. That Merry Mayhem doesn't actually mean anything to you anymore." She glances at Nora. "No offense."

Nora looks like she's in actual pain. "She can still care about Merry Mayhem without caring about Sam."

"Exactly," Violet says. "And that's what I'm going to do."

"What do you mean?" I ask.

"I'm going to do Merry Mayhem without Sam. I guess *against* Sam," my sister says, her chin tipping up.

"You…are?" I ask.

I love my sister very much. She's eight years younger than me. Our two brothers are between us, but Violet and I are still very close. I've always felt very protective of her, and I'd do anything for her.

Except tell her that she could do better than Sam.

I never did that. And I should have. She absolutely could have done better than Sam. And I swear if he'd ever proposed or something, I *would have* said something. I just kept thinking they were young and that there was no way she was going to settle for *him*.

But she did. For four freaking years. And when he broke up with her, she was distraught. Absolutely miserable. For *months*.

If he had ever come back and tried to reconcile, *then* I would have done something.

Told him off. Punched him. Locked her in her room. Set his car on fire.

You know, something reasonable that would have made the point.

But he never did. He never came back. As far as I know, he never sent her even a text.

In fact, he immediately started dating Ashley.

Soon after, he brought her home to visit, and I ran into them here in Perks and Rec. And I did something very out of character —I told him he was not welcome and to never set foot inside my grandfather's restaurant again.

He must have believed me because he hasn't. Neither has either of his brothers.

I'm pretty proud of that, actually. I'm not really a boat-rocker. Especially in our small town.

I own a business here. I have a daughter in school. My whole family lives here.

If I go around making threats and pissing people off, it can have big consequences. So, I tend to bite my tongue a lot and quietly stew, or vent to Andi and Nora. But I don't *do* things that might make the town upset with me.

I definitely would have made an exception with Sam, though, if I'd needed to.

Violet wasted so much time on him.

"How are you going to compete against Sam in Merry Mayhem?" Andi asks. "Don't you need a partner?"

"Yep," Violet says. "I've got one." She gives us a big smile.

"You…do?" I ask.

"Who?" Nora leans in.

Violet's smile grows. "Remember the guy I went to that wedding with?"

"The wedding where the two women knocked the cake over?" Nora asks.

"Yep." Violet nods happily. "We've been texting, and he agreed to come here for Christmas and to do Merry Mayhem with me."

"But…" I start. She's told us *nothing* about this guy. "You're dating him?"

She turns away to grab another beer for someone. She flips the top off and then hands it over the bar. "We haven't done anything since the wedding, but he's so great," she says. "He's charming and sweet, and he's *so* good-looking. He said he's happy to come for Christmas."

The wedding in October was the first time she'd really been out with anyone since the break-up. I'd been so relieved she'd actually gone and that it had been fun. I'd had no idea they were still talking, though. She hasn't said a thing about him since the morning after the wedding.

But she's gun-shy after Sam. I get that. When she and Sam broke up, it affected both families, too. Our parents have all known each other for years and years, and Sam felt like part of the family, as much as I'd hoped it wouldn't be forever.

But I like this idea. I like the idea of Sam seeing her with someone new. I love the idea of her having the chance to enjoy Merry Mayhem. I hated the idea that she'd have to be a spectator this year instead of a participant. It's not my thing, but Violet loves our town's crazy celebrations.

This is good. Great, even. She can jump right back in and see that the holiday fun she's had in the past wasn't about Sam. She can make new memories. She can move on.

And she and the new guy can kick Sam and Ashley's asses.

"Okay," I say. "Well, great. I can't wait to meet him."

She smiles. "He's going to call later and we'll make a plan for tomorrow."

"Great!" Nora says, hopping off her stool. "I'm so glad you're good," she tells Violet. "I've gotta go, though. So much to do!"

"Sure. I'll see you later," Violet says.

Andi and I both stand too. "I need to go pick Ruth up from Jordyn's," I say.

"Aren't they on Christmas break?" Violet asks.

"Oh, yes, they were decorating cookies." My twelve-year-old and her friends are so excited about Merry Mayhem, but they couldn't wait until the kick-off party to start on holiday treats.

Andi points at Violet. "Call me if you need anything."

"I will. But I won't need anything!" Violet says. "I've got this, you guys, I promise. I've got a plan, and *nothing* is going to derail it. Merry Mayhem is all mine!"

I'm feeling good as we head out.

I really want Violet to be confident, secure, and happy.

If this new guy is the answer, then great. I will welcome him with open arms.

And unlike what happened with Sam, I will be honest with my sister about how I feel about this guy from the very start.

CHAPTER 2
JOSH

"YOU CAN NOT BE SERIOUS! You're breaking this off right before *Christmas*?"

The cute brunette behind the bar paces to the other end before whirling and stomping back toward where I'm sitting.

"This is *such* a dick move!" she exclaims into the phone she's holding to her ear. "I went to the most annoying wedding *ever* with you! You *owe* me!"

She stops right in front of where I'm sitting, but she's not focused on me. She's staring over my shoulder, and I assume she's picturing whoever's on the other end of this call. From the murderous look on her face and the way she's holding the knife she was previously using to slice limes, I'm *very* glad it's not me.

She's probably five-five or six, *maybe* a hundred pounds. She's wearing leggings and a long flannel shirt with knee-high boots that have a two-inch heel. Her long dark hair is gathered into a ponytail. She's very pretty and doesn't *appear* dangerous.

Unless you look directly into her eyes at the moment.

I shiver. She wants someone's balls on a platter.

"This was the *agreement*!" she says. "You *promised*! What am I supposed to do now? It's in *two days*!"

I look down at the best shrimp po'boy sandwich I've ever had.

And that's saying something. The woman who cooks at the restaurant where I usually eat is a hell of a cook. I'm not that partial to po'boys generally. They're a little boring in my opinion. Not that I'd ever even think of uttering such a thing inside the borders of this state. Jesus, I'm not an idiot. But when there are things like muffalettas or jambalaya or even just red beans and rice, why would I go with a plain sandwich like a po'boy? All of those other things are far superior. But this one? It's the remoulade sauce. It's gotta be. Or the seasoning on the shrimp. Or the breading on the shrimp. Or all of the above. The bread is pretty fucking good too.

I want another bite, but it feels a little rude to keep eating in front of the bartender while she's clearly getting dumped right before Christmas.

That really sucks.

I can relate.

Kind of.

Sure, I was dumped like eighteen months ago, not just before Christmas, but still.

Actually...can I call it a dumping when we weren't really together, and Sierra just finally officially told me it was never going to happen and that she'd fallen in love with someone else?

Sure, *felt* like a dumping.

Not that I had anything to compare it to. I'd never been dumped before.

But it had *really* sucked and had been followed by three nights of booze and wallowing in my feelings.

I don't remember the wallowing, but the people around me finally got sick of it and told me about it when they said I'd had enough time and needed to pull myself together.

And then there was three months ago when she'd gotten married to the guy.

That had sucked a lot, too. My friends had given me another twenty-four hours of drunken wallowing, but not a second more.

They claimed that I should have already been past that from the eighteen months prior.

They probably had a point.

"Asshole!"

I'm pulled from my thoughts of Sierra by the bartender slamming her phone down on the bar right by my plate.

"Oh shit!" She immediately picks it back up and checks the screen. She sags in relief, then gives me a sheepish smile. "I can't afford to replace another broken phone. I just got this one after throwing my last one at the wall."

I lift a brow.

"I'm not nice to phones. That's what my mom says. Right after she says no, I can't have or borrow money to replace whichever one I just smashed."

"There's been more than the one against the wall?"

"One with a shoe. Broke the heel on the shoe too. That I *extra* regretted. And there was one I threw at a TV. Broke the TV too, but it wasn't mine and he deserved it, so I didn't regret that."

She smiles.

Well, that's something. I didn't smile for a week after Sierra dumped me.

It *was* a dumping. Come on. Telling a person that it's never going to happen between you when you've known the person for years, know the person *followed you to another state,* and is obviously in love with you? That qualifies.

"Oh, and I ran over a phone once," the bartender adds. "But that phone wasn't mine, so I'm not sure if I should count that."

"Well, that wasn't being nice to the phone," I point out.

"True." She grins. "Do you need a refill?"

"Sure."

She tops off my soda.

"Anyway, sorry about that," she says, waving toward her intact phone. "I've been waiting for him to call and tell me what time he'll be here tomorrow." She shakes her head and mutters, "Fucker."

"Uh, no problem," I tell her. "Sometimes you just gotta deal with the shit as it comes up."

I'm the only one sitting at the bar. It's just past seven on December twentieth. We're in Louisiana, so it's not like the weather is bad, but I've gotten the impression in the twenty minutes I've been here that the town is all home getting ready for the big Christmas festival that starts tomorrow. There was the usual dinner rush here in the coffee shop-slash-diner-slash-bar, but everyone headed out after eating rather than hanging around.

Perks and Rec is an interesting establishment. It's a coffee shop from six a.m. to four p.m., then a bar from four p.m. until midnight. The front door invites people to "perk up" in the morning and then "recreate" in the evening.

But they take it even further. Half of the building—actually including the outdoor patio—is decorated in bright colors—yellow, pink, and white—and holds bookcases, a coffee bar, and a bakery case along with overstuffed upholstered chairs and round white bistro tables. The other half features dark blue walls and ceiling, twinkle lights, a slate gray floor, high granite-topped tables with a fully stocked bar, and a corner stage.

They serve food all day, but the menu changes from breakfast and light lunch options to dinner at four.

I'd come in after the man I'd come to town to see hadn't answered his phone. I'd shown up in town unannounced, so that's my own fault. But I know this place is his husband's, and I'd hoped maybe Harley would be here. Nope. It's just me, the bartender, and a couple of women having drinks across the room.

I've never visited Harley at home. We've been texting for the past six months. The last time I saw him was at the hospital the day before he was discharged. I'd visited him three times during his eight-day stay after his stroke. I never do that with people I meet because I'm the paramedic on the ambulance that responds to the call where they have been injured or are having some kind of medical emergency. But Harley was different. I'd felt compelled to go check on him in the hospital. I'd ended up staying and visiting with him for two hours that had just flown by, and when he'd invited me back, I'd gone.

Tonight, when I'd been feeling melancholy, I'd thought of Harley and thought, why not stop by and see how he is? But I hadn't made plans with him ahead of time. I'd just shown up and then texted to see if he was around. He hasn't answered.

I'm just feeling restless.

Christmas is coming in four days, and I won't be with my family this year, as I was just home for Thanksgiving.

I don't mind that, actually. I love my family, but my siblings are all married and having kids. My mom and dad are so worried about me not doing those things, especially after I stupidly packed up and followed Sierra to Louisiana. *Not* being there at the most nostalgic time of the year is a favor to them, honestly. I'll let them revel in my three siblings doing things the right way and allowing my dad to play Santa and my mom to craft her butt off.

My perpetual single status can be out of sight, out of mind, hopefully.

My mom won't hang my stocking, all by itself, at the end of the row of stockings, and sadly stroke it, wondering if I'm going to die alone.

My dad won't wrap my gifts, including the extra ones they buy in an attempt to fill the supposed holes in my heart and life with material things, while being sad that he's not wrapping stuff for *my* kids.

My brothers won't ply me with liquor in an attempt to keep me tipsy and, hopefully, not sad. Because Jesus, my middle brother, is terrible with feelings.

My aunt won't bake extra everything, so I know *someone* is thinking of me.

And, most of all, my sister won't be tempted to bring single women she knows over in an attempt to set me up.

Though that one wouldn't be all bad…

No. I don't want that. I do *not* want a holiday fling back home, where I'll have to leave her on December twenty-seventh when I return to Louisiana and my life here.

A fling back home that will make my mom start hoping that I'll move back.

I'm staying in Louisiana. Even without Sierra. It's been the fresh start I needed in every way, except romantic.

I'm no longer gambling. I'm not in debt. I'm not keeping secrets from my family. I've got my dream job. I've got friends who don't come from my messy past.

And dammit, I can start over with a woman who doesn't know that messy past. Or at least, who won't judge me for it because she knows me *now*.

Sierra was never able to get over the stupid mistakes I made, and fair enough. She was evidently looking for an older, more mature, more stable type. The cardiothoracic surgeon who already has two daughters in middle school and salt-and-pepper hair at his temples, type. Apparently. Because that's what she got.

Not the younger, trying-to-get-his-shit-together, twenty-four-hour-shifts-at-a-time firefighter type. Because that's who followed her here, who turned his whole life around for her, and who laid it all on the line the day after he found out she was engaged in a massive grand gesture in the hospital emergency room.

And got shot down.

"Sorry you had to hear all of that," the bartender says.

I shake my head, forcing myself out of my own thoughts. I'm clearly not the only one facing a less-than-perfect holiday.

"Don't apologize. Sorry about your break-up," I tell her honestly. "That sucks. Especially so close to Christmas."

She shrugs. "Oh, it's okay. It wasn't really a break-up. I just don't know what I'm going to do about Merry Mayhem."

I study her. She really doesn't look sad. She no longer looks like she wants blood either. She's put down the knife.

"Merry Mayhem?" I ask.

"It's our town…" She hesitates.

"Festival?" I ask. "I heard some people talking about getting food booths and displays set up."

She grins. "Festival is such a nice, normal word for it."

I arch my brows.

"It is kind of a festival," she says. "There are displays and booths for people to buy food, gifts, and things while they watch the competition." Her face and voice have both brightened.

"Competition?" I ask.

"Oh yes," she leans in, clearly excited. "It's a three-day-long event. All kinds of things happen. Each day is something different. There's an obstacle course, a relay race, and a scavenger hunt." Her eyes are practically sparkling now. "So much!"

"Sounds interesting," I admit.

"Beats watching *another* Christmas pageant like other towns do," she agrees. "Or just sitting around with nothing to do."

I chuckle. "So, is there a money prize or something?"

"Well, there's a statue, but it comes with something even *better* than money," she says.

"What's that?"

"Bragging rights."

I laugh. "Seriously? That's it?"

Her eyes widen, and she straightens. "Around here? That's everything. We take our competitions and victories *very* seriously."

"Well, I'm sorry your boyfriend is going to miss it."

She frowns, then her gaze drops to her phone, and the frown eases. "Oh, him." She sighs. She looks side to side, then asks, "Can I tell you something?"

"Sure."

"He wasn't my boyfriend."

"Oh?"

"Yeah." She sighs. "Want the whole story?"

"Definitely." I find that I mean that.

"Okay, this is the fifth year for Merry Mayhem. My cousin Nora came up with it when she took over as the director of the

Parks and Recreation department. And my boyfriend Sam and I have won the past *four* years."

My brows climb. "Wow. No kidding?"

"Seriously. We were unbeatable. But..." She swallows. "Sam broke things off with me just before Valentine's Day this year. Right before our fifth anniversary."

"Damn."

"Yeah. I was devastated. And now..." She's running her finger along the edge of the paper placemat in front of me. "He's coming home for Christmas with his new girlfriend, and they're going to be partners for Merry Mayhem."

That definitely sucks.

She lifts her eyes. "I swear, if he wins this year with a new girl, it will be the ultimate humiliation. Everyone always said we were so good because we were soulmates. If he comes in with a new girl and wins, that negates everything we had. And yeah, we broke up and whatever, but it would be nice to think that while we were together, it mattered. It was *four years* of my life." She presses her lips together. "I don't want to think that it was all just...nothing."

God, please don't cry.

The situation is definitely messy. And I don't blame her for being upset. Four years is a long time. I had a thing for Sierra for two, and *that* seems like a long time. I was convinced we would end up together. We weren't *together*, but I had plans. I can't imagine what it would feel like to have four years be for nothing.

"I'm really sorry," I say again.

She then leans closer, bracing her forearms on the bar.

I lean in a little too.

"So...I did something a little crazy."

I really want to hear this. "Like what?"

"I found someone to pretend to be my boyfriend."

I blink at her.

"Chad was perfect for this," she goes on. "Super good-looking. In great physical shape. Would have been *amazing* at the obstacle course and stuff. Charming, funny—he would have been great with things like Christmas Carol Karaoke. You get points from the audience voting, so even if you suck but really ham it up and make the audience love you, you can still win." She blows out a breath and leans back. "But the dickhead decided he needed to be home with his family instead." She frowns. "Even though I held up *my* end of the bargain and went to that stupid wedding with him."

I shake my head. "Wow. That's..." Two men have let her down now. "...worse than my holiday situation."

She laughs lightly. "Thanks, I guess?"

"Just all sounds really fucked up," I say.

"It is," she agrees. "For one, that wedding was *soooo* bad. These two women got into a fight, and one of them pushed the other into the cake. The whole thing collapsed, and they rolled around in it for almost five minutes before anyone pulled them apart! So, I didn't even get cake out of the deal."

Uh...wow.

"And my family is expecting me to bring someone home." She's staring at something over my shoulder again, thoughtful. "They're already so worried about how I'm going to handle this Christmas without Sam. They were really relieved when I told them I was bringing someone new home. So was I, honestly. I don't want to run into him around town alone. Now..." She sighs sadly.

An idea hits me. It's a little over the top. But it might be exactly what I need. And I think it's what she needs to.

I need a distraction. I need some fun. I need to not be at home, but I also need to avoid Autre, my new hometown, where everyone will try so hard to include me and make me feel less awkward about being the only one without family.

A crazy-fun Christmas competition a few towns over sounds like a great time.

"Well, what if—" I start.

"Are you single?" she asks at the same time.

I nod. "I am."

"What do you do for a living?"

"I'm a firefighter and paramedic."

Her eyes widen. "Like you can carry a whole human being up and down a ladder with full gear on?"

I nod again. "Yep."

"What are you doing for the next three days?"

I grin. "I think I'm helping you win Merry Mayhem."

Her grin is wide and bright as she extends her hand across the bar. "Hi, I'm Violet."

"Hi, Violet. I'm Josh."

"It's *really* nice to meet you, Josh," she says with a huge smile.

CHAPTER 3
JOSH

"HEY, Michael, I'm in New Orleans. Won't be back until really late."

"Everything okay?" my friend, and Fire Chief, asks.

"I'm fine. But I am at St. Michael's," I say, naming the biggest hospital in New Orleans. We know the entire ER staff here. "I came upon a car in a ditch and pulled the driver out. I'm here with her now."

"Oh, shit. She okay?"

"She will be," I say, taking a deep breath.

"Good to hear. Let me know if you need anything."

"Thanks. I might need some time off."

"Whatever you need."

"Thank. I'll fill you in lat—"

"Oh my *God!*"

I whirl toward the door to the room.

"Ma'am, I really need to inform the doc—" The nurse following the woman into the room is cut off by the rest of the people barreling into the room, all talking at once.

"Violet!"

"Oh my God, she's *unconscious?*"

"Violet? Honey, can you hear me? Violet!"

"Ma'am, please don't shake her!" the nurse says, alarmed.

"What are all these machines for?"

"She's definitely unconscious!"

"Oh my *God*!"

"What did they tell you on the phone?"

"They just said she was in an accident and was here, and we needed to come!"

As the group fills the room, I step back, pressing against the wall across from Violet's bed. "Uh, Michael, I'm gonna have to let you go." I hang up without waiting for his response.

There's a woman who appears to be in her fifties. She's got dark hair that's pulled back into a messy ponytail at the base of her head. She's gripping the hand of a man whose brown hair curls around the collar of his shirt. He's wearing a jacket over his button-down shirt. He's studying the monitors above the bed and isn't saying much.

There are two other older men with them. One is short, round, and has a bushy white mustache that goes with his bushy white hair. He's also wearing bright pink cargo pants with a pink and white Hawaiian shirt, and pink boat shoes. The other is taller, bald, and has a neatly trimmed goatee. He's now demanding to see a doctor.

"Sir, I've paged the doctor. She'll be here as soon as she can, but we really need to hold the noise down."

"My granddaughter is lying here in a coma! We deserve some answers!" the bald man exclaims.

"Oh my God, do you think she's in a *coma*?" the woman asks.

"I'm Dr. Thurman Lafitte," the man in the Hawaiian shirt says. "Who is the attending physician?"

"You're Violet's physician?" Kristy, the nurse, asks.

"I'm retired now," he says, "But I brought that baby girl into this world. I demand to know what's happening."

Kristy clearly isn't sure what to do. I step forward. "I can maybe be of some help."

Kristy seems to notice me for the first time. She looks relieved. "Oh, thank God, you're still here."

"Okay if I fill them in?"

She glances at the family, then back to me. "Sure."

Typically, this would be the physician's job, but I know exactly what's going on with Violet. This family is obviously about to erupt, and honestly, keeping them calm and providing them with information is more critical at this moment than who gives it to them. I'll keep it superficial.

"Are you a doctor?" the man, who called Violet his granddaughter asks.

"I'm not. I'm a paramedic. I'm actually the one who found Violet and brought her in."

They all turn to face me at once.

"You're the one who found her?" the woman, who I'm going to assume is Violet's mother, asks.

The nurse, Kristy, jumps in then. "He came upon Violet's car accident. Probably saved her life. If he hadn't found her, who knows how long she would've been out there."

The woman gasps and covers her chest with her hand. The man, more Violet's mother's age—possibly her father—, looks a little pale.

I shoot Kristy a look. She's exaggerating. Violet would not have died. She was unconscious when I found her, but she was breathing and was not bleeding, externally or internally, from any injuries. She'd hit her head very hard, however.

Her mother steps towards me. "Thank God for you. Thank you so much for saving my daughter."

"Just doing my job, ma'am," I tell her. "But I'm sure it's what anyone would've done if they discovered her car."

"What happened?" Dr. Lafitte asks.

"That wasn't entirely clear. There were skid marks on the pavement, and her car was in the ditch, upside down. I'm going to assume she tried to swerve to avoid something. There were no other vehicles or any animals, however. She hit her head and was unconscious when I found her. She's been unconscious since."

The woman casts a worried glance toward Violet. "What's happening? What's wrong with her?"

"She's stable. But I am going to say something that's going to sound really scary, and I promise you it sounds worse than it is," I tell them all.

They all nod their understanding.

"They have her in what's called a medically induced coma."

The mother and her grandfather gasp again.

"A coma?" her dad asks.

"Yes, but it's been induced and is being monitored closely. They can bring her out of it at any time. They're doing it to let her brain rest and give her a chance to heal. It will just be for a day or so."

They all look at Dr. Lafitte for confirmation, and he nods.

"Nothing else is wrong?" her mother asks.

I shake my head. "Nothing broken, no internal injuries. She's going to have a hell of a headache when she wakes up and will have to go through a concussion protocol. But she's going to be okay."

They all sag with relief almost as one.

"Thank God," her mother says again.

The man pulls her into a hug. Dr. Lafitte puts his hand on Violet's grandfather's shoulder.

"What road was she on?" Dr. Lafitte asks.

"Um…I'm not sure the name of it," I admit. "It's a back road. I was on my way from Rebel to Autre."

"Maybe she was going to New Orleans?" her mother guesses.

"She said she needed to get some things for Merry Mayhem," I offer. I understand that not having details about an accident bothers people. It helps calm them when they have the whys and hows."

Her mom turns fully toward me. "I thought you said she's been unconscious this whole time?"

"She has," I confirm. "I was at Perks and Rec earlier tonight. We were talking about Merry Mayhem and…"

They've now all turned to face me, their faces full of interest.

Her mother's eyes widen. "Wait, you're *him*?"

My brows arch. I'm who?

"You live in Autre?" she asks.

I nod dumbly. "Yes. For a couple of years now."

"I can't believe she didn't tell us that!" her mother says, but she's smiling widely.

Dr. Lafitte says, "Of course. Now this makes sense. They were going to drop his car off in Autre on their way to New Orleans." He steps forward and extends his hand. "Thank God you were right behind her.

I take his hand because what else am I supposed to do?

"I'm so sorry it didn't even occur to us," her mom says. "She's told us *nothing* about you! Not even your name. But oh, my goodness, it's so nice to meet you."

Who do they think…

"Wait," her dad says. "You're her new *boyfriend*?"

He's connected the dots just a second before I do.

Oh.

They think I'm Chad.

Oh shit.

What do I say here?

But wait… Her mom said that Violet has told them nothing about the new guy.

So…I guess I *could be* the new boyfriend.

It's not entirely true, but it's also not entirely *untrue* either.

We *did* make a date earlier tonight.

I didn't expect to find her upside down in a ditch on my way back to Autre, of course. But I had stopped in Bad, a town between Autre and Rebel, to say hi to a few friends and kill some time. I was just restless tonight and didn't want to be back in Autre too early. Somehow, Violet passed me on her way to, I assume, New Orleans.

I happened to come upon her car, but of course, I hadn't known it was hers until I got out and was down in the ditch assessing the situation. I would've stopped for anyone. It's part of my training, and I'd also like to think it's part of my humanity. But when I realized who she was, my heart almost stopped.

Still, it wasn't until this moment that I realized that yes, I pulled my date for Christmas out of the ditch and was now meeting her family.

Well crap.

Do I keep up this story with her family?

Looking at the woman lying in the hospital bed, I know without a doubt she isn't going to be doing so much as getting up on a ladder to put a star on top of a tree for Christmas. She definitely isn't going to participate in any obstacle courses, relay races, or anything else too festive.

Still, without her conscious and giving me cues here, I'm not sure what to do. I didn't want to ruin this whole thing for her.

"Yep, I'm Josh, the guy who was coming to Rebel for Merry Mayhem with Violet," I hear myself say. "I'm sorry we won't get to do that."

It's fine. That's not a lie. The competition would have been fun.

Her mother reaches out and grabs my arm. "Oh, you still have to spend the holiday with us."

"Oh no, that's not necessary."

"Of course it is. That was your plan anyway. We insist. Besides, you'll want to be around to hear all the news about how she's doing."

I *will* be very curious about how Violet is doing over the next few days. And it would be a very dickhead thing to say that I don't care.

"Definitely," I say.

"And you'll want to be there when she comes home," her grandfather says.

That would be nice. It's one thing I love about working in the small town now versus the city where I trained. In Autre, I do get to follow up on how people do after we intervene.

Besides, Violet seemed great. And I definitely want to know that she's doing well. "I definitely want to see her after all of this," I say.

"And we certainly want to get to know the person she's been spending time with. We know she went to that wedding with you. We'd love to get to know you better."

Yeah, I kind of stepped into this.

But I nod. Because you know what? I wanted a new plan for Christmas. I don't want to sit around and have people feel sorry for me. I don't want to do the same thing I've done for the past two years and be the twenty-seventh wheel at the Landry family celebration.

And hey, Violet and I had hit it off. It might be unusual to get to know the woman's family before I get to know her, but what the hell? If I want to keep seeing her after Merry Mayhem, having her family like me has to get me some brownie points, since I won't be able to impress her with my obstacle course agility.

"Okay," I finally say. "I'd love to join you."

Her mother smiles broadly. "Wonderful. We'll have dinner tomorrow night, and we'll talk about the plans for the weekend."

Dinner and plans for the holiday weekend sound wonderful.

"Thanks, I'm looking forward to it," I tell them honestly.

"And you can meet Thea," Violet's father says.

"Thea?" I ask.

"Our other daughter," the woman says. "Silly me, we haven't even introduced ourselves. I'm Bebe, and this is my husband, Eli. Violet is our youngest daughter. We have two boys, and our oldest daughter is Thea. We also have a granddaughter, Ruth. Thea's daughter."

"It's really nice to meet you all."

"And I'm Bruce," the tall man says. "I'm Violet's grandpa. This is Brewser. Well, his real name is Thurman. Family friend," he says of the good doctor.

"Nice to meet you, too," I say.

"The whole town loves Violet very much. They'll be so glad to meet you. We've all been worried about her," Bebe says. Her eyes fill with tears. "This is so not how we expected to spend Christmas." She glances back at her daughter. "I am so grateful that she's not seriously injured and that you were there for her." She reaches out and squeezes my arm again. "While she might be in the hospital, we'll look on the bright side. This whole thing brought you to us."

Ouch. A little pang of guilt hits me.

But I'm not lying to them or tricking them. Violet and I made a deal to spend the weekend together. I *was* going to do Merry Mayhem with her. And she had used the term *boyfriend*. Sure, the word 'pretend' had been in front of that, but I had still been prepared to play the part of crazy-about-her nice guy. If that makes her family happy, then where's the harm?

And who knows? Maybe at the end of all of this, we'll take 'pretend' off the front of that.

CHAPTER 4
JOSH

"ELLIE, I NEED SOME ADVICE."

"Anytime anything, darling," Ellie Landry tells me as she leans on the top of the scarred wooden bar in her bar and restaurant that, as far as I know, is just called Ellie's. There's no sign outside with that name, or any other, on it, though, and everything inside is plain, from the napkins and coasters to the menus, which are printed on plain paper and replaced only when they are ripped or stained to the point where the offerings are no longer readable.

That all drives her marketing specialist granddaughter, Charlie, absolutely crazy. But Charlie has yet to convince her grandmother that spending the extra money on things that tell people where they're eating is worth it.

Ellie always says, 'If they're already inside eating, why the hell do they need a napkin to tell them where they are?'

The plain napkins and coasters really match the general aesthetic, though, and I think even Charlie would agree if pressed. The place is full of mismatched chairs and tables. Even the barstools are an eclectic mix of sizes, colors, and styles. The drinkware, too. It's pretty clear that Ellie buys sets of glasses, but when things break, she replaces them with whatever she finds or likes at the moment.

The walls are "decorated" with a collection of photos of people and events Ellie loves, posters of bands and sports teams she likes (which get removed if she gets pissed at them for any reason), and, more recently, landscapes of the Louisiana bayou and wildlife photos. Again, the photos or pieces of art are added simply because they strike her fancy. There is absolutely no unifying theme, color scheme, or anything other than "Ellie".

Which makes calling the place "Ellie's" the most obvious thing.

Ellie is the matriarch of the family that adopted me two years ago when I ended up in Autre, Louisiana, the tiny Bayou town that needed a full-time firefighter after I finished my training in New Orleans.

I have to admit that landing in this little town is the best thing that's ever happened to me. Yes, I followed a woman from Omaha, Nebraska, to New Orleans, but the fact that none of the fire stations had a full-time opening at the time I was applying turned out to be fantastic for me.

Autre is a fraction of the size of the city where I grew up, but a guy thousands of miles away from home, without friends or family, still quickly found both in this quirky little town. It's not just the rest of the firefighters—almost all volunteers—at the station or my fire chief, Michael LeClaire. It's literally almost the entire town. And I'm certainly an honorary member of the Landry family.

Ellie and her husband, Leo, stepped in where I had missed having my grandparents around, and all of her kids have turned into fill-in parents, aunts, and uncles. Her grandkids are definitely like siblings.

For better or worse.

"I'm not gonna be here for dinner tonight. Or for Christmas," I tell Ellie in a hushed tone. I have to let someone know. Someone being Ellie, because I'd rather not get into it with the whole crowd.

I've already told Michael about everything and arranged for coverage, of course. We have fantastic volunteers in town and Autre, and the area will be well taken care of. Michael was a little too happy that I've got plans that involved a woman. I'm not going to analyze that. He's a good friend. He wants me to be happy. I know he'll want details later, but for now, he just said, "No problem. We've got you."

Ellie's eyebrows arch. "You planning to set something on fire to get out of Christmas? Because I have a request."

I chuckle. "You have a request for a building you want set on fire?"

"A couple of 'em."

I shake my head with a grin. "I am not setting anything on fire, and don't tell me, because if and when those buildings go up in flames, I don't want to have to include in the report that you had it out for them."

She winks. "Got it. So, what're you doin' instead of eatin' my bread pudding and pecan pie?"

I groan softly. I do love her pecan pie. "I got another invitation."

Ellie immediately gives me a knowing look. "Is she pretty?"

I grin. "Of course."

"Do I know her?" Then she waves the towel she's holding in one hand. "Of course I do."

"Actually, I'm not sure you do. She's not from here."

Ellie looks mildly offended. "Do you think the only people I know are from here?"

I should've known better. Ellie is… actually, I'm not sure how old she is. Old enough to be a grandmother to people in their late twenties and early thirties, and to have several great-grandchildren now. But she's younger at heart than some people my age. And I'm guessing no one is brave enough to actually ask the woman her age. I'm certainly not.

"Fair enough. She's from over in Rebel. Do you know anybody over there?"

She laughs. "You're hilarious."

"I don't know what that means. No, you don't, or yes, you do? Y'all have a big rivalry with them or something?"

She looks at me with surprise. "You really don't know."

"Actually, a lot of things fall under that heading. What about this specific situation do I not know?"

She laughs, and I feel a stab of pride in my chest. It's always a good day when you can amuse Ellie Landry. And an even better day when you can tell her something that impresses her or that she didn't already know.

Those are very rare days.

"Honey, I grew up in Rebel. That's my hometown."

Okay, now I'm actually surprised. "You're not from here?"

"Nope. I'm here because I fell in love with an Autre boy, which is a very hard thing to avoid doing, by the way. But I know pretty much everybody over in Rebel. Who did you meet?"

"Violet Chabert," I say.

Ellie swats me with her towel. "She's my great niece. But honey, she was just in a car accident."

I lean in, shushing her slightly. "I know. I was the one who found her in the car. But she's your great niece?" I ask, going back to that point.

"Her grandpa is my brother."

Wow. That's definitely a strange coincidence.

"You found her in her car?" Ellie asks. "She's been unconscious since then. You've developed a crush on an unconscious girl?"

"Shhh," I say again, casting a glance around.

Her grandkids are all gathered around the family tables at the back of the bar, and I'm fortunate that they are a boisterous group. There's no way they would hear our conversation over their own unless they were standing right near us.

"I met her before the accident. And we set up a little date over the weekend. When her family found out, they invited me to Christmas dinner anyway."

"Oh." Her eyes narrow thoughtfully. "Yes, they'll be wonderful for you."

My eyebrows arch. "Well, thank you."

"No, really. You'll love them. And they'll love you. You should definitely go."

"Wow, don't let the door hit my ass on the way out."

She chuckles. "I know you've been feeling a little bit left out around here. Everybody's coupled up and everything. And everything that went down with Sierra bruised that big heart of yours. I think it's great you're going to have some fun in Rebel."

I watch her for a moment and ask, "You're serious, aren't you?"

"Are you doing things a little out of order with the family before you get to know the girl? Sure. But I'm hardly one to advocate falling in love in a normal way. Where's the fun in that?"

I laugh. "Well, I think falling in love might be jumping ahead a little bit."

She gives me a wink. "I give it three days. Tops."

I have to remind myself that the Landry family is very into love. And falling fast doesn't faze a single one of them.

"Well, thank you for the confidence. But…"

I feel the need to confess the whole story to *someone* and have them tell me not to go to Rebel.

Or that it's okay.

Ellie is my choice.

Even before I knew this was her family in Rebel. Now she's even more qualified to tell me if what I'm going to do is crazy.

"But what, darlin'?" Ellie asks.

"Before her accident, when we set up the date, it was for me to pretend to be her boyfriend," I blurt out. "She had another guy who had agreed to do it, but he backed out. She wants a boyfriend for the holidays because her ex will be in town."

Ellie nods. "Ah."

"And I agreed because it sounded fun and harmless. But now she's unconscious, and her family thinks I'm this new guy in her life and… I don't know if I should go ahead with this."

"Of course you should."

I blink. She didn't even think about it. "Yeah?"

"Yes. My brother called to tell me about the accident. They were so scared."

"She's going to be okay," I say.

"I know. They know. But it was still hard to see her like that. And she's been having a tough time since the break-up. She and Sam were together for a long time. Everyone expected them to get married. The break-up was a shock. So, this is giving them some hope and happiness."

"But…it's not real."

She gives me a soft smile. "You're very real."

"But Violet and I aren't together."

"Listen, you didn't make this up on your own. You and Violet agreed to do this. Just play along. Especially while she can't be part of deciding to change it."

"But they seem great," I say. "I don't want to lie to them."

"So don't lie," she says simply. "Let them get to know the real you."

Yeah, they don't know Chad. He and Violet were not 'dating' for long. I can just play this as myself. And hope that Violet is cool with that when she wakes up.

"They're going to love you," Ellie says. "You're going to make this holiday really wonderful for that family. I appreciate that. I love them a lot."

I smile. Ellie is a firecracker, but underneath that crispy outer layer, she's mushy and sweet. Like a toasted marshmallow. "Thanks, Ellie."

She waves that away. "I have something for you to take with you." She disappears through the swinging doors that lead into the kitchen.

"JD!" someone from the Landry family table calls out to me.

I turn in the general direction. I'm JD to everyone in Autre because there was already a Josh in the family, and they decided it was too confusing to have two. They'd suggested Hot Shot, Hot Stuff, Not The Chief, which they were going to shorten to NTC, and Chief Junior, which we all know they would have shortened to Junior. I vetoed all of them. Of course, that didn't matter, but thankfully, some of the women had been on my side. Finally, Ellie asked for my middle name, and just like that, Joshua Daniel turned into JD when I'm in the city limits of Autre.

"Get over here, we're saving you a seat."

And they are indeed. The family is so large that they have their gatherings— pretty much dinner every night—at Ellie's bar. And yes, they always save me a seat. Right in the midst of them. Which is awesome. I always feel included and cared for. But I'll be honest, I'm kind of excited about having something else to do tonight.

"Actually, I can't."

"You sick?" Zeke Landry asks.

"Not sick. I have other plans."

The table goes quiet, and they all look at one another as if they don't understand the words I just said.

"Is everything okay?"

This comes from Michael, the one I probably know the best. He grew up as a friend of the family and was a Landry by default even before he married one of Ellie's granddaughters. You can't spend more than ten minutes with this family and not feel like one of them.

"Everything is great, actually," I'm happy to report.

"Well, what are you gonna be doing?" Zeke asks as if he cannot fathom anything better than hanging out with the rest of them.

And I'll be honest, there are probably only a handful of things that I would put on the list ahead of spending time with this group.

"How about I go do it, see how it goes, then come back and tell you about it?" I say.

Zeke sits back in his chair and slides his arm along the back of his wife's chair. "It's a girl," he announces to the table.

His twin brother, Zander, rolls his eyes. "Well, no shit."

They all start talking amongst themselves about me spending time with a girl that they don't know about, which means I can bow out. With the Landrys, even if you are the subject of a conversation, you don't actually have to participate for the conversation to go on.

Ellie returns from the kitchen with a pie in hand.

"You can take this."

"One of your pecan pies?" I ask.

"Yes. And by the way, I'm certain they'll have pie. Bruce is a hell of a baker."

"Then why am I bringing pie?"

"Because my pie is better. And you are not only encouraged, but are *required* to tell him that when you hand it to him." She holds it out to me, then pulls it back. "Promise me you'll say that."

I chuckle. "You're gonna get me in trouble with this family from the very first minute, aren't you?"

She grins and hands the pie over. "You're going to be fine. You've been hanging out with us for two years."

"So, they're definitely not crazier than you all?" I ask affectionately.

"Oh, I didn't say that," she tells me. "But we've been good practice for what's in store for you."

CHAPTER 5
THEA

THE SOUND of a horn honking pulls my attention to the right, and I gasp as I see the front of the red pickup only a foot away from my bumper.

I glance in the rearview mirror and realize that I just rolled through the four-way stop.

Damn. My bad.

Did he have the right of way? Likely.

Just because this four-way stop never has four cars stopping at once doesn't mean that I shouldn't come to a full and complete stop.

Just because this is my very tiny hometown and the traffic laws seem to be more guidelines than actual binding legal require-ments doesn't mean I shouldn't be paying attention while I drive to my grandfather's house for dinner.

I lift my hand in a tiny *oops, sorry* wave, and the guy in the truck waves back.

I start to proceed. But so does he. We slam on our brakes again.

I realize that it was probably his turn to go, but I'm more or less blocking his way now.

In my defense, I wasn't looking at my phone screen or some-thing. I was just lost in thought.

Sure, that's also dangerous. But I wasn't texting while driving, at least. And I'm definitely not under the influence. Not under the influence of anything other than annoyance at least. I'm trying to figure out how I can possibly see all of my patients on the day after Christmas, since they have now all asked to be rescheduled from the next two days to December twenty-sixth.

They act as if they just now realized when the dates for Merry Mayhem are.

Or just realized they want to be at Merry Mayhem.

Both of which are ridiculous.

Merry Mayhem has been happening on the twenty-second, twenty-third, and twenty-fourth of December for the past five years. And everyone in town always wants to go.

Should I have realized that these people were making physical therapy appointments with me on the twenty-second and twenty-third and that they would very likely be canceling? Maybe. But they're grown adults. Why did they sign up for those timeslots if they knew they would rather be downtown watching the obstacle course or relay race?

Okay, fine, my receptionist, Lana, probably just told them, 'See you on Wednesday' rather than pointing out that it was December twenty-second.

Life in Rebel, Louisiana, is kind of a day-to-day thing for a lot of people.

Still, everyone's been talking about Merry Mayhem for over a month.

My cousin Nora, Director of Parks and Recreation, and creator of Merry Mayhem—and a lot of the other mayhem that happens in town—has been sure that everyone is talking about this annual event.

The truck honks at me again.

I scowl at him. Then realize it's not him honking. It's the truck behind me. Because the red truck and I are just sitting in the middle of the intersection at a stalemate

I gesture for him to go. He lifts a hand in acknowledgement

and turns right. Then I proceed through the intersection, following him down Main Street.

I don't recognize his truck, and I get even more curious when he takes another right turn down the next street I need to take.

I follow him for three more blocks, and then my frown deepens as he pulls up at the curb in front of the house I'm headed to.

I pull into the driveway behind my parents' car and shut off my Jeep.

All the lights are on in my grandfather's house, and I know that I'm about to walk into a noisy, aromatic, boisterous gathering of my family. And this is just a regular weekday dinner. It's nothing like Christmas dinner will be in a couple of days.

But I'm not thinking about dinner, or my growling stomach, or the fact that I am fifteen minutes late and will hear about it from my mother and my grandpa Bruce.

They do not understand—never have, even now that my grandpa Harley is in physical therapy himself—that my schedule is dictated more by when my patients decide to show up and how long they need to rehash the latest town gossip—there's always something new—exchange recipes in the waiting area, and compare notes on their rehab progress before they get to any actual rehab.

They are all scheduled for hour-long time slots, but no one stays in my clinic for less than ninety minutes.

Of course, I can't charge them for all of that time because most of it isn't specifically physical therapy. But, as counterproductive as their chatting is for staying on my own personal schedule, I understand that their visiting and comparing notes about when their staples are coming out, and their range of motion measurements, and how far they walked the dog yesterday, all function as emotional and mental therapy, and that is just as important as the physical aspects I attend to.

"What is he doing?" I mutter as I watch the man from the red truck get out, grab a container off the front seat, then proceed up the front walk toward my grandfather's front door.

But he stops at the top of the path before the porch steps and turns toward me. As if waiting for me to join him.

I sigh and tuck my keys into the front pocket of my bag and get out. Might as well see what this is about.

"Well, hey, Danger."

"Danger? That's a little hyperbolic."

He just chuckles.

"Are you here to kick my ass for the stop sign situation?" I ask from beside my car.

"Of course not."

"You want an apology?"

"You gave me the *oops, sorry* wave," he says. "Though I did think it also meant *go ahead, I'll wait.*"

I roll my eyes. "So, can I help you with something else?"

"I don't need any help."

I decide to go ahead and get closer. "So why did you follow me here?" I ask. Then I move so that I can see him more clearly in the shadow of the tree, and I stop. "JD?"

He straightens. "Thea?"

"Uh...hey."

I know this guy. He was one of the paramedics who showed up when my grandfather had his stroke *as we were driving home* in June.

He gives me a big grin. "Hey! It's nice to see you again."

"Yeah, you too."

It is. It *really* is. He's a very charming, sweet, heroic, good-looking firefighter and paramedic whom I've thought about more than a few times since that horrible day back in June. He'd been calm and competent and had taken care of my grandfather and my daughter, who'd hit her head when the car had come to a jerking stop as Harley had realized something was wrong and had pulled over and slammed on the brakes.

And he had taken care of me. He'd been comforting even while he'd been totally honest about what was going on and what could happen to Harley before they got him to New Orleans. He'd seemed to know exactly the words and tone to use with each of us. When to be gentle, when to be firm, when to be funny, and when to just acknowledge our fear.

I'll admit I'd asked about him afterward.

My cousin Ami's husband, Michael, had been the other paramedic to show up, and so I'd asked her about him three days later, when I'd found out he'd been up to visit Harley in the hospital.

But she'd told me he was hung up on some woman he'd followed to Louisiana from Nebraska.

I'd let it go.

Sort of.

I hadn't tried to get his number or run into him. But I had sent brownies to him at the fire station in Autre. They had been *thank you for saving my grandfather's life* brownies, not *it would be okay if you called me* brownies. Who sets up a date with a stroke patient's granddaughter, right? That would have been weird.

But when I'd found out that he'd been up to visit Harley twice more and had played checkers with Harley and taken him on walks and smuggled in some of Harley's sister's bread pudding, I developed a little crush despite myself. I mean, I'm thirty-one. Can I have a *crush* on someone? Maybe not. I just don't know what else to call it.

"Why are you following me?" I ask, trying to sound flippant, when, in reality, I'm shocked to see him, yet very pleased.

"Uh, *you* followed *me*." He tips his head. "Are *you* here to kick *my* ass?"

I smile at him. "No. And I'm running late, so I wouldn't have time even if I wanted to."

"That's a relief."

I feel my smile grow. "So, whose house are you looking for?"

Why is he here? If he knows one of Harley and Bruce's neighbors, I'm going to be so annoyed that I've missed all of his other visits.

"Bruce's," he says, glancing at the big red front door with the enormous wreath on it. "This is it, right?"

"You're coming to Harley and Bruce's house? Why?"

"Dinner." He frowns and steps forward. "Wait, Harley? This is Harley's house? As in Harley, your grandfather?"

"Yes. His house and Bruce's." I frown and step forward. "You didn't know that?"

"No. I..." He shakes his head. "I knew Harley's husband's name was Bruce, but I didn't make the connection between this Bruce and that one."

He's dressed perfectly for dinner at my grandparents' house. He's in scuffed, but clean, brown work boots, blue jeans, and a T-shirt under an open light flannel shirt. His dark brown hair is cut short and slightly mussed on top, and he's clean-shaven. He's probably about six-two or three and trim with broad shoulders and thick biceps.

He looks just as good as he did in that uniform he'd been wearing when I met him in June.

"So, you just met Bruce? Randomly? Separate from Harley?"

"Well, yes. I mean it was—"

"You're finally here!" my dad exclaims from the open door.

We both turn to look at him.

"And Josh! You made it."

"Hi," JD greets with a smile.

"Josh?" I ask.

"My name's Josh. I only go by JD at work."

Ah. Okay.

And my dad knows him, too. This is such a weird coincidence.

"Thanks for the invite," JD—Josh—says, smiling broadly at my dad.

"I see you two met," my dad says, stepping onto the porch and motioning for us to come inside.

"Yes. Previously." Josh turns and motions for me to precede him up the steps.

"And how do you know J—Josh?" I ask Dad.

"We met at the hospital when we were visiting your sister," Dad says, taking the container Josh is carrying and starting for the kitchen.

They met Josh at the hospital?

That's…random.

But I think I understand what's going on here.

Josh and I pause in the foyer to kick off our shoes. I brace my hand against the wall and say softly, "I'm really sorry about this," as I lift a foot to untie my tennis shoe.

"About what?"

"Them talking you into this dinner."

"They didn't talk me into it. I was happy to be invited," he said, setting his boots side by side next to the rows of other shoes.

He must not know what this is. He must think this is about Harley. This is so embarrassing.

I toe off my other tennis shoe and look down. I'm in leggings and a polo shirt from my PT clinic. My hair is in a ponytail, and I'm sure the little bit of makeup I put on this morning is worn off by now. I *know* I have nothing on my lips, and I definitely didn't bother with eye makeup. It's a physical therapy clinic. People come to me hurt and sick. They don't care if I'm glammed up.

Besides, everyone I treat has known me all my life. Or all of theirs. The teenagers who get hurt playing football or basketball come to me for their rehab, just like their grandparents see me after their hip replacements and heart attacks, and their moms come in for my pelvic floor strengthening class.

I don't need mascara to make these people do ten more reps of their hamstring curls.

But if I'd known my family was setting me up with a guy they met at the hospital while visiting my sister, I *might* have put on some Chapstick in the car.

And if I'd known it was JD—*Josh*—from June, I would have done better than Chapstick.

"But did they tell you *why* they invited you?" I ask Josh.

He straightens and runs a hand through his hair.

I have to tip my head only slightly to meet his gaze, but I'm five-seven, so yeah, he's probably six-two or so.

"I assumed it was because they wanted me to have dinner with them," he says with a half-smile.

Oh, confident. Okay, then.

"This is a setup," I say.

His brows arch. "Is it?"

"Yes."

"Between...?" he asks.

"You and me."

"Huh."

He doesn't seem surprised. "Did they tell you that?" I ask. Maybe he wanted to meet me? I feel a little warm swirl in my belly, and that needs to *not* happen.

Does he know I have a kid? Not just a kid but a *pre-teen*?

The last time I tried dating was when she was a toddler, and frankly, it sucked. Either men bolted as soon as they knew about the I-come-with-a-kid-thing or they thought we would just do "our thing" on the side, minus the kid.

Ruth is the most important thing in my life, and *every* relationship I have involves her. I don't bring people into her life casually.

Which is why I haven't dated in... God, so freaking long.

"Did your family tell me that this dinner was a set-up between you and me?" Josh asks.

I nod.

"No, they did not."

I sigh. "I'm sorry. They try this once in a while. Whenever they meet a nice guy that *they* like, they try to set him up with me or my sister." I frown. "Though my sister is very rarely single. So, it's usually me."

"How do those usually work out?" he asks.

"Not well."

"Why's that? Your family actually has terrible taste?"

I smile. "Maybe."

"Well, then—"

"Mistletoe!"

He's cut off by Ruth sliding on stocking feet into the foyer and pointing at the arched doorway above us.

"Hey, Ruth," Josh says. Clearly, he remembers her. That's nice.

"Hi!" she says enthusiastically. "Grandpa said to come get you."

"We're coming," I tell her, taking a step forward.

"But, mistletoe!" she says again. She points.

I look up. And roll my eyes. I know Harley, put that there and caught Bruce under it, and Bruce groused about silly traditions, but let himself be kissed and secretly liked it.

And I notice no one pulled the mistletoe down.

Because they're trying to set me up with this good-looking, laid-back firefighter paramedic they picked up at the hospital where my sister is in a coma.

"We're *not* doing the mistletoe thing," I tell her.

"You *have* to," she informs me. "Just kiss on the cheek."

"You *have* to," Josh says softly behind me.

I turn. "You don't really—"

But he leans in and presses his lips to my cheek.

Licks of heat ignite from that spot and tickle down my neck, across my nipples, and make more heat twist through my stomach.

Damn, he smells really good.

Like pine and soap and Christmas cookies.

Okay, that last part is probably coming from my grandpa's kitchen, but it's why I close my eyes *briefly* and breathe deeply.

The *only* reason.

"And by the way, I'm here because of Violet," he says gruffly near my ear before straightening.

I blink up at him. "Uh…what?"

"Come *on!*" Ruth says, spinning and heading for the kitchen.

Josh's looking at me with a hard-to-define expression. "This isn't a setup between you and me. I'm your sister's date."

And isn't that just exactly what a woman wants to hear while her nipples are tight and tingly from a simple kiss on the cheek?

CHAPTER 6
JOSH

WELL, that escalated quickly.

I hadn't even set foot inside Violet's grandfather's house, and I was already second-guessing the plan to pretend to be her boyfriend.

Because of her sister.

This is a little messy.

Violet is cute. Beautiful even. I'm attracted to her in the way that a straight single guy is attracted to a beautiful woman. Objectively, I know that she's beautiful and that kissing her would be pleasant.

But when I met her, I did not experience a slap-me-across-the-face-till-my-ears-ring-and-I-don't-know-which-direction-is north-hot-lust-and-need.

I did with Thea.

In June.

And I've thought about her multiple times since then.

I did *not* go visit Harley in the hospital, hoping to run into her or to try to get information about her. In fact, I got zero information about her from Harley, and I was okay with that.

But I've still thought about my friend's granddaughter more than makes sense, considering I met her while her grandfather was having a stroke, spent time with her in the back of an ambulance and a hospital emergency room, and haven't seen her in six months.

But I can confirm now, seeing her again, that saying I'm attracted to her is like saying the ocean is a little damp.

This is going to be a problem.

I am now sitting across from her at her grandfather's dining room table, eating one of the best meals I've had in a long time—not that I would *ever* admit that to Ellie—wondering what the fuck I'm going to do about this.

I'm your sister's date. Really? *That's* how I decided to explain to her what I'm doing here.

But it's the truth. It's not like she wouldn't have found out within five minutes at this table because it's all her family has been able to talk about.

Thea has now been regaled with a story of how I came upon Violet's car accident, pulled her to safety, took her to the hospital, and sat by her bed until the family showed up.

They've also all exclaimed over what a small world it is and what a wonderful coincidence it is that I was the paramedic to save both Harley and Violet.

My mini-reunion with Harley was awesome. He was so happy to see me that I got a little choked up, and his hug was solid, demonstrating that he's definitely gained strength and improved his balance since I last saw him.

We laughed over the fact that I never made the connection between Ellie's brother and Harley. Ellie never used Harley's name when talking about her brother, and Harley never told me his sister now lives in Autre.

When he was in the hospital, long, in-depth conversations were difficult. He'd lost some of his speech ability at first, and we'd stuck to easy topics, yes and no answers, and playing checkers—which he could move with his unaffected hand—and walks.

Since then, our text messages have consisted mostly of check-ins, comments about Nebraska football and New Orleans hockey, our favorite sports, and the occasional funny meme. It's more to show that I'm thinking of him, and when he responds, I know he's doing well and still making progress with his cognitive and fine motor abilities.

Thea's trying to avoid eye contact with me now.

I wish I knew what that meant.

"So, you know Ellie?" Ruth asks me.

"I sure do. I've been living in Autre for a couple of years now. I see Ellie every day."

"I love her," Ruth says enthusiastically. "And Leo. He's here a lot."

"Is he?" I hadn't realized that.

"Leo and Harley are best friends," Ruth says. "I mean, besides Bruce," she says, looking at her great-grandfather Bruce.

He winks at her.

"Well, Leo's my brother-in-law," Harley says.

"What's that mean?" Ruth asks.

"He's married to my sister. So, by law, he's my brother," Harley explains. "But really, Leo would be like my brother even without the law."

Ruth smiles. "You and Bruce were friends before you married him. What was that called?"

"Just friends," Bruce says, reaching for the rice. "He was married to your great-grandma for a while before we got married. That's how your grandma and uncles and everyone came to be."

"Before great-grandma died, right?" Ruth asked.

Bebe nods. "Right. Bruce was always a good friend. Then, after my mom died, slowly Bruce and Harley realized they loved each other more."

"Well, it wasn't so slow for me," Bruce says with another wink. "It took your great-grandpa a little time."

Ruth has clearly heard this story before. She just smiles and keeps eating.

"You've known Ellie and Leo a long time, too?" I ask Bruce.

"Grew up with Ellie and Harley," he says with a nod. "And I've known Leo since he and Ellie met."

"You're not *from* Autre, though?" Bebe asks me.

"No. I'm from Nebraska. Grew up in Omaha."

"You're a long way from home. What brought you to Louisiana?" she asks.

Oh boy. Well, I'm supposed to let them get to know the real me. "Honestly," I say. "A woman."

I shoot Thea a glance. She's watching me now.

"Really?" Harley asks. "What happened there?"

He doesn't seem a bit apologetic about asking.

"I followed her here when she relocated for a job."

"Were you engaged or something?" Ruth asks.

"No. We weren't even dating. But I was crazy about her."

Everyone smiles at that. Ah, they *are* related to the Landrys. Everyone in Autre loves my love-sick story as well.

Okay, everyone except Thea smiles at that.

Her eyes are back on her plate now.

"What happened?" Harley asks. "You're not together now, obviously."

"She got married a few months ago," I say.

Bebe gasps.

Harley leans onto the table and points his fork at me. "Please tell me you at least told her how you felt."

I nod. "Yes, sir. I showed up at her work the day after he proposed to her and declared myself in front of an audience of about thirty people. Flowers, her favorite ice cream, and a big diamond ring. Told her she had options."

Bebe is covering her mouth now.

Bruce is also leaning in. "What did she do?"

"Turned me down flat," I say with a nod. "That was well over a year ago."

"Would you say that you're prone to going over the top?" Harley asks me.

I think about my past poker addiction, some of the stupid shit

I'd done with the money I'd won—I'd been *very* good at poker—the way I'd uprooted my life to move to Louisiana in one day, the way I'd showed up at Fire Academy the day training started basically begging them to let me in, and the way I'd jumped into this situation with Violet.

I nod at Harley. "Yes. I'm afraid so."

He grins. "Then you're going to fit in just right around here."

I chuckle.

"Was the wedding you and Violet went to in Autre?" Thea asks me. Or technically, she asks the collar of my shirt because she's not making eye contact.

Okay, I don't want to lie to them. So far, so good. But now, how do I answer this?

"The wedding wasn't in Autre, no," I say. That is true. However, I have no idea where the wedding was. But there were no weddings in Autre in the past month.

"Sounds like it was a doozy," Bebe says.

I grin. "Really embarrassing for two grown women to end up on the floor wrestling in a wedding cake, isn't it?" I say, repeating the story Violet told me.

Again, not a lie. That did happen at the wedding Violet went to, and that *is* embarrassing.

Harley laughs. "Embarrassment is all in the eye of the beholder," he says.

"Some people deserve to be thrown into a cake," Bebe agrees.

I chuckle and can't help but watch Thea's reaction.

She rolls her eyes, but there is a smile teasing her lips.

"It's rude," Bruce says. "Someone spent a lot of time on that cake, presumably. They could've thrown each other into the macaroni and cheese. That's a far easier thing to put together."

Thea's father sits back in his chair, grinning. "So, you're not opposed to people throwing each other into food. It's more about which food?"

"Coleslaw," Harley says. "Coleslaw is a big ass mess, but it's not a lot of effort to make. *That's* what you throw someone into if you're trying to make a point."

"What was the point?" Ruth asks. "Weren't they just mad, and pushed each other, and the cake happened to be there?"

Bruce puts a hand on his chest. "Well, I certainly hope not. That's an even bigger travesty. That poor cake is just a victim, then."

"Agreed. If you're going to push someone around, you have to be aware of your surroundings," Bebe says. "You want it to be messy and uncomfortable, to do a number on their clothes and to make it difficult for them to just walk out nonchalantly, but you don't want it to be something dangerous."

"Like the table with the forks," Harley says, nodding.

I snort and again look at Thea. Her smile has grown, but she is still simply taking bites of crawfish étouffée without comment.

"Well, forks, of course," Bebe says. "But I was thinking that you want to avoid hot dishes. Or things that will stain."

"If you're mad at someone, why do you care if the food stains their clothes?" I have to ask.

"Well, of course, it depends on who it is. But the chances are you're going to be over it in the morning. You don't want to damage their clothes permanently. Like gumbo. That would stain. Or barbecue ribs—those not only have sauce that will stain, but those ribs could poke someone somewhere they shouldn't get poked."

"Where *should* someone get poked?" Eli asks.

"Well, I—" Bebe starts.

"Butt cheek," Harley says.

"Butt cheek," Bruce says at the same time.

They look at each other and both say, "Exactly."

I look at Thea again. She's definitely laughing silently, and now she meets my gaze.

We share a grin, and I feel heat spread all the way to my bones.

"Anywhere else has the potential for damage," Bruce says.

"Agreed," Harley says.

"Cake wouldn't damage anything," Eli says.

"Still… the cake doesn't deserve that," Bruce protests.

"But the macaroni and cheese would be hot," Bebe says.

"I'm telling you, coleslaw," Harley declares.

"So how did you and Violet meet?" Thea asks me, obviously trying to change the subject.

Okay, so some of this is going to be tricky. "Right place at the right time," I say with a little shrug and a smile.

Her mother beams at me, so I know that's a good answer.

"I was at Perks and Rec, and we started talking. Hit it off right away," I say, also not lying.

"I can't believe you've been to Perks and Rec and I've never seen you," Bruce says.

"Guess the timing's just been off," I say. I know I'm insinuating I've been there more than once, but I haven't *said* that. "Love your shrimp po'boys."

Bruce grins.

"It's the remoulade sauce," Harley tells me.

"The seasoning in the breading is also excellent," Bebe says.

I knew it.

"Anyway, Violet was telling me about Sam and about Merry Mayhem. Sounded like a hell of a good time, and I wanted to try it out, so she asked me to be her date."

"She told you about Sam?" Bebe asks.

I nod. "Yeah. He sounds like a jerk."

Bebe looks a little sad. "He's really not. Or he wasn't. He felt like a son to us."

Oh, damn.

Thea scoffs but doesn't say anything.

"I know you're mad at him," Bebe tells her daughter.

"I am," Thea agrees. "He broke my sister's heart. He broke all of your hearts," she says to the table. "Of course I'm mad at him."

"I saw him downtown yesterday," Eli says. "He was with his dad. He looks good."

"I'm dreading running into him," Bebe admits. She looks at

me. "Sorry. He was just a part of the family for a long time. Both families thought we were going to be one big family eventually."

Yikes.

"I get it," I say. Damn, he made all of these people sad, not just Violet. This crush-Sam-at-Merry-Mayhem really would have been fun. "I'm sorry it might be uncomfortable." I think fast. "Violet really didn't want him to win Merry Mayhem this year. You know, the first year it wasn't the two of them together."

Bebe nods.

"So, I'm still going to do Merry Mayhem," I announce. "For Violet. To keep Sam from coming in here and claiming the title. Especially with her in the hospital and everything."

Everyone straightens in their chairs.

"Aunt Violet is going to be home in time for Merry Mayhem?" Ruth asks excitedly.

That takes the smile off everyone's face.

I hate that. "No, she needs a few more days in the hospital. But she might be home for Christmas Day. Or soon after. She's going to be okay," I say firmly. "I talked to the doctor and the nurses I know on the floor. They say she's stable and there are no concerns." I look at her parents. "Of course, you might've gotten a more detailed report."

Bebe nods. "Yes, we were up there this morning and saw the doctor. But he said the same. Things look good. They're hoping to wake her up the day after tomorrow."

"But she won't be ready for things like Mayhem," Eli says quickly to Ruth. "She's not going to be up for running around and climbing, and all of that craziness for a while."

"That makes sense," Ruth says. "But who are you going to do Mayhem with?" she asks me.

"Oh, I'll just do it on my own," I say. "I can handle it."

"The rules say you have to have a partner," Ruth says.

Oh. I look around the table. "Really?"

They all nod. "It's a partner competition," Eli confirms. "Teams of two."

"Well, Ruth, what do you say? Wanna be my partner?" I ask.

Ruth is clearly touched and excited by the invitation, but she shakes her head. "I'm not old enough. It has to be somebody eighteen or older."

"Well, I'm sure I can get somebody from over in Autre." However, I'm not sure who. They'll all be busy with Christmas stuff.

"Mom can do it," Ruth says.

Everyone looks at Thea.

My pulse quickens. I'm not sure why. Just the merest *hint* of the *idea* of me and Thea spending some time together? Wow, I've never reacted to a woman like this. This is wild.

She's already shaking her head.

"Oh, no. I'm not… I have to…" But she trails off and then sighs. "Dammit, I can't come up with an excuse fast enough."

Everyone around the table laughs.

"You really can do it?" Ruth asks, bouncing on her chair. "You've never done it, but you go every year. You know all about it! You'd be so great at it!"

"Especially the cookie eating part," Thea says, grinning at her daughter.

Ruth laughs. "Yes! But seriously, Mom, that would be *so cool* if you did it!"

Thea blows out a breath. "My schedule at the clinic actually just cleared out," she says, obviously a little annoyed by that.

"Clinic?" I ask.

"My mom is a physical therapist in town," Ruth says. "Everyone wants to go to Merry Mayhem, and *nobody* wants to go to physical therapy."

Thea sighs. "It's true. I'm not busy, and these people would probably be dragging me to all the events anyway," she says, gesturing around the table.

"And you definitely don't want Sam to win," Bruce says.

"And you love eggnog," Eli says.

I meet her gaze across the table, again feeling that bone-heating effect. "I could definitely use you then. Not a huge fan of eggnog."

She sits back and crosses her arms, studying me. "Fine. But just so you know, I'm going to use the entire time to get to know you well enough that I will know every phobia, allergy, and weak spot you have so that if you do anything to hurt my sister, I will be able to make you regret it very, *very* much."

I grin. "I look forward to it."

CHAPTER 7
THEA

I NEVER LIKED SAM.

My family would never believe that. He was a nice guy. Solid. Decent. Seemed to make Violet happy. And he and I always got along when he was around.

But I knew she could do better.

As evidenced by the guy who is sitting at the table making my grandfathers laugh, my parents beam, and my daughter chatter excitedly about Merry Mayhem.

Sure, Ruth is always excited about our town's crazy annual Christmas competition, but her animation for the event has tripled now.

Because Josh is not Sam.

He's better.

So much better.

I rinse another plate and load it into the dishwasher. Starting the dishes was the perfect excuse to get out of the dining room and away from Josh.

Sitting across from him for dinner had been...stupidly distracting.

I don't get distracted by men. That's ridiculous. I'm thirty-one. I own a business. I have a pre-teen daughter—God, Ruth will be thirteen in two months, how did that happen? I'm a grown woman who interacts with all kinds of men in all kinds of settings all the damned time. I never get *distracted* by any of them. Amused? Sure, sometimes. Pissed off? Definitely. Annoyed? All the time. Charmed? Okay, on occasion. But distracted? What. Is. That?

How can sitting across my grandfather's dinner table from a younger guy—he can't be more than twenty-five—who is *dating my sister* make it so I don't remember what we even had for the meal I just finished?

Fuck. Josh, the guy I've been thinking about on and off for *six months*, is *dating my sister*.

It's a very weird coincidence. He didn't even know Violet and Harley were connected.

But dammit. Why did he and Violet have to meet and hit it off?

I have to get *over* this crush that I'm definitely too old to have.

But as I brace my hands on the edge of the sink and squeeze my eyes shut, I can picture the shape of his mouth, the color of his eyes, the way his hair falls over his forehead, the way his hand and fingers look wrapped around a glass.

I run the back of my hand over my forehead. Do I have a fever or something?

Am I just horny?

Maybe I should get my hormone levels checked. It's early for perimenopause, but anything is possible, I suppose. That makes more sense than me being smitten by some guy.

I hear a deep, warm laugh from the dining room and squeeze the scrub brush a little tighter as I scrape rice and sausage into the garbage disposal.

I really like his laugh. And *that* is ridiculous, too. But it's deep and rich and real.

Josh is still in the dining room with my family, and I can hear everyone talking and laughing. He's enjoying his time with my family. He seems completely at ease, and they're all happy to have him here.

I run water into the cooking pot and add soap. I need to scrub something. Hard.

Because I like him. And I barely know him.

He was there during one of the scariest days of my life. I would feel this way about any guy who had been there when my grandfather had been having a stroke. This is just a strange hero-worshipping thing I have going on. It's not real. I just remember him as competent and gallant because of the situation.

And every guy looks good in a uniform.

I'm not *actually* attracted to him.

I just like him because he was very kind to my grandfather.

And he's my *sister's boyfriend*.

I *should* like my sister's boyfriend. That's okay. It's good, even.

But I should *not* get a hot swirling sensation in my belly when he laughs.

I scrub the side of the pan, enjoying the feel of the friction and the heat of the water. It stings the hangnail I have on my middle finger, and I welcome that as well. I deserve that. *You should not lust after the guy your sister is dating.*

So...I'll just ignore the warm swirly feelings he causes. *Hot, they are definitely hot, swirly feelings.* Ugh. I'll ignore *all* the freaking feelings he causes. We're going to be partners for Merry Mayhem. That's it. I'll just be grateful I'm not Sam's partner in Violet's place.

Oh, grateful? That's what you're going to feel? Really?

I scrub harder.

So what if Josh is respectful of my grandfathers and didn't even blink about them being gay? Or that he's kind to my daughter. Or that he also didn't seem to think twice about me being a single mom and didn't ask about Ruth's dad, even in a roundabout way. He's taken everything in stride. He's been charming and seems fully comfortable with my parents.

But so what? So what if, as a firefighter and paramedic, he's probably seen a lot of shit, people at their worst, some strange, not great circumstances, and is programmed to help, rather than judge? Unlike Sam, who is a finance bro and hangs out exclusively with other finance bros and not only judges people down on their luck, but also judges people who drive cars that are more than three years old.

And so what if Josh is genuine and warm and even…sweet? I guess that's the word.

Sweet is good. Violet deserves sweet. She deserves to see a major contrast to what she had and know that there are other options out there. She also deserves someone who loves her family.

We all do.

I'm not heartbroken that my family thought Sam would be a part of us and then ended up breaking up with all of us. I'm heartbroken that Sam never really loved my family the way he should have.

I was glad when they broke up. I didn't like seeing my sister upset, of course, but I haven't missed Sam. I was glad to hear he had a new girlfriend. Hopefully, that will keep him the fuck away from Violet while he's in town.

The way Josh shared the story about how he followed a woman from Nebraska all the way to Louisiana shows that he's far more romantic than Sam ever was. The way Josh admitted that he tends to go overboard at times shows he's at least a little self-aware. The fact that he seemed a little sad and even embarrassed that the woman chose another man over him showed that he's got some humility. He didn't seem angry or even jealous. He seems a little heartbroken, which is…nice. It's nice to think he's got a heart and cares about this woman, but also respects that she chose someone else and moved on.

Plus…he's really hot.

I squirt more soap into the pan and scrub harder.

It doesn't need it, but I do.

It's okay to think my sister's boyfriend is a good guy, but is it okay to think he's hot?

Maybe. It's maybe just an objective fact, and my observing it is just…something anyone would do.

I need to talk to my girlfriends. I need them to see Josh and see if they also think he's hot.

I look around for my phone. It's lying on the counter several feet away. I look down at my sudsy hands. Dammit.

I need to text Andi and Nora and let them know they have an extra assignment tonight at the Merry Mayhem kick-off event. Nora will definitely be there. It's her event after all. But I need to be sure my grumpy, divorced friend Anderson will show up. She usually does for Nora's stuff, but all this holiday craziness makes her roll her eyes extra hard.

I rinse my hands and grab the faucet sprayer to rinse the pot.

The hose reminds me that Josh is a firefighter.

Firefighters are automatically hot. It's not just me. I'm certain Nora and Andi will agree. Firefighters are freaking heroes. They're willing to run into burning buildings to save other people, for fuck's sake. That's definitely sexy.

And he's willing to do Merry Mayhem to help Violet save face in front of Sam.

He doesn't even really know what Merry Mayhem is or what it entails.

Dammit. I like Josh.

Violet definitely upgraded.

So I like him. So what? That's good. And I'll just—

"Hey, what time should I be here tomorrow?"

I gasp and whirl, still gripping the sprayer and showering Josh with water.

The stream hits him directly in the chest.

The plates he's holding don't even wobble.

He just looks down at the water, then back up at me, one eyebrow quirked.

I drop the sprayer and grab a towel, stepping forward and starting to blot at his shirt.

Standing this close, I can smell him again—still really like it—

and I am very aware of his size. Also, how hard the chest muscles are behind the wet shirt I'm stupidly trying to dry with my mother's dish towel that has Christmas lights embroidered around the edge and says *Christmas Calories Don't Count* in the center.

He clears his throat and grabs my wrist, encircling it with those long fingers I noticed at dinner. I freeze with my hand and the towel against his chest.

"Don't worry about that," he says, his voice a little gruff.

He leans closer, and I suck in a little breath.

But he's not leaning closer. He is leaning *around* me to set the plates that he's holding on the counter behind me. Then he takes the towel from my fingers and blots at his shirt himself.

"I don't think this is going to work," he says.

"My brothers have some stuff upstairs. I'll get you something."

"Thanks."

Neither of us makes a move to put more distance between us.

One part of my brain is screaming at me to step back. But another part, the part that was just running through all of the reasons he seems like such a great guy, which is also the part right next to that part that was very annoyingly asking why he had to stop into Perks and Rec on a night Violet was helping out rather than one of the nights I was filling in (i.e., the part I have been stubbornly refusing to acknowledge) is yelling louder. And that part is saying *stay right here*.

I swallow. "Um, you asked me a question when you came into the kitchen?"

I'm *very* proud I was able to remember that.

He nods. "Yeah, what time should I be here tomorrow?"

That part of my brain that I've been trying to ignore notes that he doesn't move back even now.

Which another part of my brain notes is maybe a red flag since he is supposed to be into my sister. I want her to be with a guy who is *all about her*.

But we're going to ignore that part too.

I'm also ignoring the part of my brain that tells me I actually know neuroanatomy, and there are not this many parts of my brain.

"Oh, well…we'll get a schedule when we go downtown tonight."

"We're going downtown tonight?"

"We have to go down and sign up to compete. It's a whole thing. A kick-off event. Everyone has to sign up, and they introduce the competitors to the town."

"Oh. Yeah, we should do that."

We should. That will make this official.

I will be *required* to spend time with this guy.

I'm feeling like a really bad sister right now because that gives me butterflies.

This is such a bad idea.

"But the thing is," I say. "The schedule is really erratic. There will be events scheduled at certain times, but they also have surprise challenges where they just text us and tell us that we have to meet somewhere, or go do something, and then report to a central location. We're not going to know when those might come in."

He chuckles, and the curl of heat in my stomach simply cannot be ignored.

"You're kidding."

I lift a shoulder. "The word mayhem is right in the title."

He nods. He's still smiling and dammit…my attraction to him is *not* my fault.

Probably.

I really need Andi and Nora to confirm that, though.

"So, Autre is forty minutes away, give or take," he says. "That could be complicated."

I nod. He's not wrong. "Last year, Violet and Sam got a text at six a.m. saying they needed to gather all of the ingredients to make sugar cookies and then report to the community center kitchen for a bake-off. At that time of day, no stores were open, and a lot of people were in bed, so if Bruce hadn't already had everything available, they would've been in trouble. One pair had to make no-bake cookies. They did get points for being resourceful. And one team frosted graham crackers."

"Did that count?"

I nod. "Half the points. For the decorating. But another team just didn't get any points because they couldn't pull it all together."

He lifts a brow. "Wow. Brutal."

"That's what I'm saying."

"And how long did they have to get to the community center?"

"An hour."

He blows out a breath. "I guess I need to get a hotel room."

"Don't be ridiculous," Harley says as he comes into the kitchen carrying a handful of silverware and a few glasses. "There won't be any hotel rooms available. Everything is booked up."

With another person in the room, I am now able to step back from Josh. It's like the magnetic force between us is broken. I should probably feel relieved about that, but I don't. Which is a huge red flag.

Another huge red flag.

Then I think about what Harley just said. Dammit, he's right.

"Yeah, things probably filled up weeks ago."

Josh's eyes widen. "This really is a big deal."

Harley laughs. "Course it is. Nora doesn't do anything small."

"Well, he can just stay in one of your bedrooms," I say to Harley.

Bruce comes into the kitchen carrying more dishes. "Sure, but it would be a lot easier if he just slept in Violet's room."

I freeze, turning back to the sink.

It definitely would be easier. We could be called to do a challenge at any moment. Every minute could count because most of the challenges have a time limit.

The problem is that Violet's room is at my house.

"I don't want to inconvenience anyone," Josh says.

"You won't. That will be *more* convenient. If you want to win this thing, every minute matters," Bruce says, rinsing off the dishes he carried in.

"Well, okay. You all have keys to Violet's place?" Josh asks.

Hartley chuckles. "We do. But you can just go with Thea."

Josh looks at me. I take a breath. "Violet lives with me. She has since February, when she and Sam broke up, and she moved back here from New Orleans."

Understanding dawns on his face. And for just a moment, I think maybe he thinks this isn't a great idea either, and maybe for the same reason I do.

Does he feel the heat between us? That could be good. Then he'll understand why we have to resist it.

It could also be bad. We need to *not* have heat between us. It will be a lot easier to ignore if I'm the only one feeling it. If it's just a figment of my imagination. Or it's just my attraction to him, and it's not reciprocated.

"Oh, well…" He trails off, clearly not sure what to say.

But I am a grown-up. I am a single mom. I am doing Merry Mayhem for my sister. With her new boyfriend. This is not weird, this is not a problem, I can handle this.

"It's fine. In fact, it's a great idea. Like Bruce said, every minute matters."

His shoulders relax a bit. "Okay, well then, thank you. I need to run back to Autre to get some stuff. I don't have any other clothes here."

Harley and Bruce seem to have just now realized that the front of his shirt is dripping wet.

I've been successfully ignoring the way the cotton has been clinging to his chest and abs.

His very firm, clearly defined through the wet shirt chest and abs…

Okay, I've been *mostly* successfully ignoring that.

"We have some clothes for the boys upstairs. I can get you

through tonight. But you can run back to Autre after the kick-off event," Bruce says. "That won't be too late for you, will it?"

"No, that's fine," he says. Josh looks back at me. "As long as you don't mind me coming in late?"

I shake my head. "Ruth is on school break, so she likes to stay up late. And now that I don't have any patients scheduled in the morning, I don't have to worry about getting up early. Unless we get some kind of Mayhem challenge."

"Come on, I'll get you a new shirt," Bruce says, turning on his heel and heading out of the kitchen.

Josh casts me a glance.

"We'll leave for the kick-off event in about twenty minutes," I tell him.

"Sounds good."

He follows Bruce out of the room, and I take a deep breath.

No, it doesn't sound good. It sounds like this could be very complicated, and I'm a bad person. Or at least a bad sister.

Because I watch my sister's boyfriend's ass as he leaves the room with my grandfather.

Merry Mayhem is already living up to its name, and it hasn't even kicked off yet.

CHAPTER 8
JOSH

THEY TOLD ME THAT NORA, the director of Parks and Rec who created Merry Mayhem, doesn't do things small.

But I wasn't ready.

We walk downtown from Bruce and Harley's place. We take it slow so that Harley can keep up with his cane—which is shaped like an upside-down hockey stick—in one hand and his other arm linked with Bruce's. But there isn't a moment of silence as we walk. The family talks and teases nonstop. They make me miss my family, and I have the sudden urge to call my family and introduce them to the Delaunes and Chaberts. They'd all get along famously.

Thea sends Ruth ahead to clear the sidewalk of any sticks, stones, or other debris, and I find out that Thea is Harley's PT. I also find out that Harley isn't as compliant as he should be. But their banter about it is good-natured and full of exasperated affection from both of them.

As we near the center of town, I can hear Christmas music, laughter, and conversation. I can also smell what I can only describe as "carnival food". It's definitely popcorn and kettle corn, but there is the mingled scent of cinnamon—churros, perhaps?—and other fried foods.

We step onto Main Street near an enormous hot chocolate stand.

I mean *enormous*. Not only are there five people pouring and handing over paper cups of classic chocolatey hot cocoa, but there is also a line for white hot chocolate and spicy hot chocolate made with chili powder. There's also a line where people can have Irish Cream, Kahlua, peppermint schnapps, or butterscotch schnapps added to their cup.

Next to the serving lines is an impressive display of toppings from good old marshmallows and whipped cream to peppermint sticks and sprinkles to cherry syrup.

Finally, at the end, is a plethora of treats to go along with the drinks. Cookies of all kinds, Rice Krispies treats, cupcakes, and more fill the multi-tiered display trays.

And it's all free.

"Wow," is all I can say.

Thea smiles up at me. "Yeah. And this isn't even officially mayhem."

I laugh.

People linger about the tables, sipping and munching, chatting, laughing, clearly in a merry mood.

The rest of the street is just as festive.

There is a huge Christmas tree at one end of the street, and at the other end, near the Welcome to Rebel sign, is a ten-foot stone statue that is also decorated for the holidays with a Santa hat on its head and lights draped around its neck.

But the statue is not the founder of Rebel, or a beloved mayor, or a famous person from Rebel.

It's an otter.

Yes, an otter. As in the animal.

Between the otter statue and the tree, Main Street is lined on both sides, in front of the storefronts for all the businesses, by booths that are just being set up and decorated, but many are offering samples of what they will be selling over the next couple of days. Some are food booths offering a variety of items, from breads and pies to candies and jellies. Others feature handcrafted goods that make great last-minute Christmas gifts, such as soaps and lotions, wood carvings, or knitted items. Other booths offer services like massages, house cleaning, and landscaping.

"Things will be in full swing tomorrow, but tonight is a chance to window shop and make a list for what people want to come back for over the weekend," Bruce tells me. "Some of these booths have been here every year, and others are brand new this year." He points at a booth selling jams and honey. "That guy drives four hours to be here."

"Wow. This is impressive," I say.

"It's a lot of fun," he agrees. "Nora is very good at her job." He beams with pride.

"Clearly."

As we stand in line for hot chocolate, people greet Harley, Bruce, Thea, and Ruth with waves and smiles.

Ruth ends up enfolded into a group of girls and promises her mom she'll be home right after the kick-off event ends.

A man approaches Thea and shows her how well his knee is bending. She praises him and then reminds him that she expects him in the clinic the day after Christmas, despite his wonderful range of motion.

A woman approaches and asks a question about her shoulder.

After we get our hot chocolates—classic chocolate with marshmallows for Bruce, chocolate with a shot of Bailey's for Harley, white chocolate peppermint for Thea, and white chocolate with caramel for me—we start down Main Street.

Another woman stops Thea and requests that she give the woman's son a mini-lecture about using his crutches even when he's out with his friends. The teen rolls his eyes, but he nods dutifully as Thea scolds him gently.

It's clear the entire town knows and appreciates this family, and Thea obviously is an integral part of this community.

"How long have you been practicing here?" I ask her.

"Since I graduated," she says. "It was always my plan to come back here and open my practice." She takes a sip and side-eyes me. "So, six years."

"What's that look for?" I ask.

"I'm thirty-one."

"Okay." I'm not following.

"Old."

I laugh. "Thirty-one is old?"

"How old are you?"

"Twenty-six."

She nods. "So, a lot older than you."

I'm not sure why she's pointing out our age difference. "Five years isn't 'a lot'," I say.

"Violet is twenty-three."

I lift a brow. "Good to know." I guess. Why is she telling me this?

"Sam is twenty-three also," Thea says.

I'm amused even though I have no idea what we're doing here.

"Sierra is thirty," I say.

Thea pauses with her cup partway to her mouth. "Who's Sierra?" She sips.

"The woman I followed to Louisiana."

Thea chokes on her drink of cocoa.

I smile and take a drink of my own.

Hmmm. She wasn't expecting that I'd be into older women before. Well, older *woman*.

Until now.

I'm definitely into Thea Chabert.

Which is, admittedly, not ideal.

But Violet and I are not involved. Yes, I need to play a part here and at least stall until I can talk to her and work things out, but Violet isn't my girlfriend, and I've made no promises to her beyond this weekend.

Thea doesn't say anything about my revelation about Sierra. She just keeps walking. And I follow. For now, I'll let her lead the way. I can't *do* anything about my attraction to her at the moment.

But I know she feels the chemistry. Our moment in Bruce and Harley's kitchen was not one-sided. Her hand on me, even while blotting my wet shirt with a dish towel, had sent fire licking through my veins. She was affected too. I saw it in her eyes.

We *are* going to figure out what this is.

But not right now. Not in the middle of Main Street, where the entire town has seemingly gathered.

Still, I'm staying at her house this weekend. It sounds like we'll be spending most of the weekend together. This is going to be even better than just a nice distraction from my holiday melancholy.

Right in the middle of the street, which is shut down from traffic, is a stage where Nora Delaune herself is presiding over the sign-up for Merry Mayhem. She doesn't look smug or frazzled. She looks like she's having the time of her life as she hands out clipboards to the people in front of her.

I climb the six steps behind Thea.

"Thea!" Nora exclaims, bouncing to her feet. "What are you doing here?"

"Hey, honey." Thea leans over the table to hug Nora. "I'm here to sign up."

Nora audibly gasps. "You're doing Merry Mayhem?" She's clearly delighted by this idea.

"I am. In Violet's place."

Nora's very expressive face immediately falls. "Oh my gosh, I went up to see her. She actually looks pretty good. I mean, for someone who's in a coma."

"She's going to be okay," I feel the need to insert.

Nora turns wide, interested eyes to me. "That's what the nurses told me."

"Nora, this is Josh Evans. He's Violet's...b...boyfriend."

I definitely notice the way she stumbles over that. Interesting.

"They were going to do Merry Mayhem together, and I'm taking her place," Thea finishes.

Nora's smile is bright and quick. "Oh wow, Josh, it's so nice to meet you. You're the one she went to the wedding with."

How to answer, but not lie? "That wedding was wild," I say. There. I didn't say yes. And that wedding did sound wild.

"Well, I'm so glad you're both doing this. Violet would be thrilled. She loves Merry Mayhem." Nora says it with a touch of pride.

"It was almost all she could talk about the other night," I say, again able to be honest.

Nora looks pleased. "She *is* the reigning champion." Then she frowns. "Sam has already signed in." She tilts her head to her left.

"Tall guy in the blue shirt," Thea fills in for me.

I spot him immediately. Sam is tall. Probably about six-three. His light brown hair is cropped short, and he's dressed in jeans, tennis shoes, and a long-sleeve T-shirt. The woman next to him, who I'm going to assume is Ashley, the new girlfriend, is very pretty. And also nearly the opposite of Violet in appearance in every way. She's curvy and at least five inches taller than the petite Violet. She's wearing bright red pants with a forest green sweater, and her short blonde hair falls in spiral curls to her shoulders.

"We can totally take them," I say to Thea.

I have no idea if that's true. These two could be secret ninja warriors.

"Oh, a rivalry," Nora says. "I love it."

Thea bends over the sign-up form and starts filling in blanks. "Do I get a family favor and a promise that you won't make us do anything before nine a.m.?" she asks.

Nora laughs as if she's joking.

I'm going to take that as a no.

Thea moves to the side. "Here, fill in your information," she says, sliding the clipboard to me.

I bend over the form, curious what information they need. First, it's the standard name and telephone number. The form explains that it needs to be a number where they can text me and where I'll be checking messages regularly. I presume for the surprise challenges.

The rest of the form asks for things like food, allergies, phobias, and anxiety triggers.

I look up at Thea. "Your quest for information about me just got a lot easier."

She grins at me. "You thought we were going to play Twenty Questions?"

I laugh. But I guess I had kind of hoped so.

Dude, this is your supposed girlfriend's sister. You need to cool it. For this weekend, at least—or until Violet wakes up and you can come up with a new plan—you need to be interested in Violet.

But I'm not. I don't dislike Violet, but I'm not curious about her the way I am about Thea.

That's not fair, you've barely spent any time with Violet.

But honestly, I have probably spent as much time with Violet as I have with Thea, and I find Thea impossible not to want more of.

This is definitely going to be messy.

The bottom of the form, in very tiny print, is a disclaimer form.

"Basically, you can't sue us for anything," Nora says in her perky voice. "You're coming into this knowing that you might get hurt, you might get sick, and you definitely might not win."

"I might get sick?"

"I can't control how you might react to copious amounts of eggnog or sugar cookie frosting," she says.

Honestly? Fair enough. I sign my name at the bottom and date it. I straighten. "Okay, I guess we're officially Merry Mayhem participants.

Thea nods. "Guess so. You can head over to Autre now if you want to."

Nora gasps again. "No, you can't leave. We're going to introduce you to everyone. And then there's the first challenge."

"There's a challenge *tonight*?" Thea asks.

Nora nods happily. "Yup. This one will help the town get to know you and set the stage for the teamwork it's going to take for the rest of the weekend."

I'll admit, I'm intrigued.

"We have a couple more teams to sign in. Go have some more hot chocolate and relax. Browse the booths," Nora says with a wave of her hand.

Thea sighs. I chuckle.

"Hey, if we're going to kick ass and bring home the trophy, we're going to need to be all in," I tell her. "Enthusiastic about all the challenges."

"You're right," she says. "It's just that three hours ago, I had no idea I was going to be doing any of this. I've watched Merry Mayhem for four years, but definitely just as an amused observer. I think it's crazy. You don't really know what you just signed up for."

I grin at her and realize that, whether I like it or not, whether it's a good idea or not, I'm looking forward to this. And it has everything to do with this woman. I get to spend time with her. Do fun Christmas activities with her. It's not just about avoiding feeling left out and sad over in Autre, I am excited about this. And I'm grateful.

I stop as we walk back down off the stage. Light glints off an object sitting on the end of the table.

"Is that the trophy we win?" I ask.

She nods. "Yep."

The trophy looks exactly like the statue at the end of Main Street.

"It's an otter, right?"

"Yup."

I follow her down the steps. "You all just really like otters?"

"There is actually more of a reason than that," she says. "I know you're from Autre, and over there, they think they are the ones who are otter crazy with the animal park and everything. But we claimed otters as our obsession a long time ago."

I chuckle. The animal park in Autre is something. It started as a petting zoo. Actually, from what I hear, it started with just a couple of otters who adopted the Landry family when they were only running the swamp boat tour company. But it slowly grew into a petting zoo, then into an animal park, and is now a full-fledged animal sanctuary for several endangered species.

There are giraffes and penguins on the bayou because of the Landrys and Autre, Louisiana.

I'm not kidding.

"So what's the story there? Why otters? Like to the extent that you put up statues?" I asked.

She opens her mouth, then shuts it and shakes her head. "Honestly, that's probably a story for another time."

I laugh. "Fine. Just get it in your head that you and I are taking that little otter trophy home. All in." I hold up my closed fist.

She gives me a fist bump and laughs. "I'm ready."

I love her laugh. I love that she's doing this. I love how this entire thing has transpired.

I said all in, and I mean it.

I haven't been *all in* on something since I packed my car one Saturday at eleven p.m., kissed my mom's cheek, and headed for Louisiana with no warning to Sierra…or anyone else.

That was two years and a whole new life ago.

But it's me. It's how I do things. I've tried to be more level-headed, contain my spontaneous urges, and not just jump in with two feet and a wish.

Fuck that. That hasn't worked out for me so well, so I'm back to all in.

I don't know if Thea Chabert is really ready for *my* all-in.

But I have a whole weekend to get her there.

CHAPTER 9
THEA

"SUGAR COOKIES WITH FROSTING OR WITHOUT?"

I think for a moment.

Josh is definitely a frosting type of guy. I'm not sure how I know that, but it feels right. So I write *without* on the little white-board I hold in my lap.

"Okay, show us your answers!" Nora says into the mic she's holding.

We all—the twelve people sitting on the stage in the middle of Main Street, the six pairs who will be competing in Merry Mayhem—turn our boards to show the audience our answers.

There are cheers and groans, and we all lean to look at our partners' answers.

I was right. Josh said frosting.

"You like *plain* sugar cookies?" he asks, mock-horrified.

"I like *all* cookies," I say. "But given the choice Nora just gave, yeah, without."

That's a total lie. Of course, I would choose frosted sugar cook-ies. With lots of colored sugar and sprinkles, too. What am I? On a cleanse?

Actually, even when I'm trying to reduce my sugar intake, I'd still take frosted sugar cookies with sprinkles over plain ones. I'm no heathen. And skip the cookies? Please.

However, these questions are designed to help the town get to know us and demonstrate how well-matched each pair is. It's not like we have to be fully in tune, of course, but this is fun for the observers.

So far, Josh and I are a perfect match.

We'd both choose hot chocolate over eggnog, wrapping gifts versus gift bags, and now this cookie question. I pretended to like eggnog better, and now blew the cookie question, though. We can *not* seem perfect for one another. He's Violet's boyfriend.

Violet does like eggnog better, is totally a gift bag girl, and hates frosting, though.

I shut down those thoughts.

So what? It's not like those things are actually important in a relationship.

The laughter and chatter around the sugar cookie question quiets, and Nora asks, "Real tree or artificial?"

Okay, this one is easy. I'm a busy, working, single mom. I really like having an artificial tree. It's much less of a mess, and I can just pull it out of the closet, prop it up, and, thanks to buying one that's pre-lit, plug it in and be done with everything but the ornaments. And I love decorating it with Ruth. We make home-made pizza, put on a Christmas movie, and decorate together one night in early December.

Josh, on the other hand, has to be a real-tree guy. He's rugged and surely has no problem using an ax. He probably goes out and chops his own down.

So, I can answer this one honestly and be the opposite of him.

I wipe "plain" off my board and write "artificial" in red marker.

"Okay, time!" Nora says. "Let's see your answers!"

We all turn our boards toward the audience.

I lean to look at Josh's answer. "No way."

"Oh, absolutely," he says. "Artificial trees are much safer.

They're generally made of flame-resistant materials. Real trees get dry and are much more of a fire risk."

Of course. He's a rugged *firefighter* who can swing an ax because he's a *firefighter*.

"Next!" Nora announces. "Christmas gifts on Christmas Eve or Christmas morning?"

All the contestants lean over their boards, but I have to think for a second again. This one is a little tougher. Is Josh the type to not be able to wait for something he really wants, or does he like building anticipation? Does he like to just jump into the good stuff, or does he like to drag the fun out?

And why is my mind taking those questions into *completely* dirty and inappropriate directions?

But it definitely takes me too long to stop the thoughts of *is he against the wall, can't even make it to the bedroom type, or would he tease and tempt and take it slow?*

I tip my head back and groan.

I hear a deep chuckle to my right.

"There's no right or wrong. There are pros and cons of each."

Oh, God, that's for sure.

I look over at him.

Both.

He'd be both.

Sometimes he'd tease and tempt and build it all up, and sometimes he'd just not be able to wait and would make a woman feel like she was the most irresistible thing he'd ever seen. Or tasted.

I slam my eyes shut. Jesus, where did *that* come from?

"Okay, time!" Nora calls.

I quickly answer the question, scrawling a word on my whiteboard without thinking. It's just a silly game before three days of silly games. I have to stop making this a bigger deal than it is. I have to stop making it about things it's not about.

Josh and I are going to spend some time together, sure, but it will all be very public, and a lot of it will be happening outside, so we'll be wearing extra layers of clothes, not fewer. No bare skin.

No worries about me getting distracted by his shoulders, pecs, and abs...

"Yes!" Josh laughs and holds up his hand, palm toward me, fingers spread.

I look at him with confusion. Then I look at his whiteboard. Where he wrote "both".

I look down at my board. Where I also wrote "both".

Oh my God.

He grabs my wrist and lifts my hand, slapping it against his in a high five.

Nora is laughing into the microphone. "That wasn't an option!"

"But we answered the same way anyway," Josh says with a grin. "Definitely a perfect pair!"

What was the question again? Not sex against the wall versus long, slow, teasing sex on a bed...

Oh, right, gifts on Christmas Eve or Christmas morning.

Well...yeah, both.

Nora shakes her head and grins at the audience. "Well, I guess we know to keep an eye on those two. Rules don't seem to matter."

Everyone laughs, but I stifle a groan. Rules *do* matter. Especially the one about *not* developing a crush on your sister's boyfriend.

Apparently, we don't receive points for matching our answers in this "get to know the contestants" challenge. We get points based on audience vote. Which is probably good. I purposefully tried *not* to answer the same way Josh did, and we still got three out of five matches.

However, Max and Mitchell, the brothers who had been dying to compete in Merry Mayhem since the first year and had only turned eighteen two months ago, matched on every single question. Big surprise, they're identical twins.

Jesse and Brad, who have been married for thirty years or more, also got every match. No big shock there.

Beckett, a hometown guy who plays for our minor league hockey team, and his sister Sutton, matched on four out of five.

But the other set of twins, seventy-something-year-old Patty and Muriel Coffelt, didn't match on a single question.

That is also not a shock.

Patty and Muriel fight about everything. *Everything*. Sometimes it's a disagreement over politics, and sometimes it's an accusation that one of them stole the other's socks. Big, small, important, ridiculous, it doesn't matter. Patty and Muriel's arguments are like white noise in Rebel. We've all just gotten used to holding onto things like lamps, paperweights, plates, and cutlery when a fight breaks out—they've been known to throw things, and we just try to keep the breakable and more lethal things out of reach.

Interestingly, Sam and Ashley only matched on two questions.

Not that it means anything. They're silly holiday questions. They don't mean anything about a real relationship.

Look at me and Josh. We're just…

What the hell are we?

We literally just met. We're not even friends. We're…

Jesus, we're future in-laws.

Maybe. I mean…

Fuck.

Anyway, it doesn't mean anything that Sam and Ashley sucked at this challenge. But it's interesting.

"Okay, just leave your whiteboards and markers on your chairs," Nora tells us. "Things will kick off tomorrow!" Jingle bells —not the song, just a cacophony of jingly bells—rings out, a muted *boom* sounds, and green and red confetti rains down on us from the confetti canon next to Nora. The crowd cheers.

"Nora loves confetti," I tell Josh with a laugh, pulling a piece off my bottom lip and brushing red and green paper from my hair.

When I look up, I freeze. Josh is staring at my mouth. I'd

worry I still had confetti stuck there, but I can feel that's not the case.

I press my lips together, but they keep tingling.

"Be sure to keep your phones close," Nora says. "The first challenge is the relay race! Right here at ten a.m.! Unless…"

I finally manage to pull my gaze to Nora.

She turns her grin to all of us. "…unless there's a surprise challenge before then! Be sure you *all* keep your phones charged and on! The next three days are going to be… *lit!*"

There's an expectant pause. But nothing happens. A few people laugh, but there's an anticipation in the air that makes everyone just…wait.

Nora frowns and looks in the direction of the tree. "It's going to be *lit!*" she repeats, a little louder.

Everyone follows her gaze.

Again, nothing happens.

"Sorry!" we hear someone yell from down near the tree. "We have a glitch! I'm on it! Just a sec!"

It's Everly Levette. The Parks and Rec department hires her company to do lawncare and landscaping for the city, and her contract also includes a lot of outdoor decorating for events, including the huge Christmas tree.

"Okay, do it again!" Everly yells again a few seconds later. "I've got it now!"

Nora snorts. "All together now! It's gonna be…"

Everyone calls out "Lit!" together.

The tree lights up with red glowing lights from top to bottom, and everyone cheers as if that was how it was supposed to happen all along.

The contestants all stand, turning over their whiteboards and making small talk.

Which means that Sam, Ashley in tow, makes a beeline for me. Dammit.

"Hi, Thea," he greets with a big smile. "Nice to see you."

"Hi, Sam."

He looks expectantly at Josh.

But he knows who Josh is. Nora introduced all of us. She even included that Josh was Violet's boyfriend, that he was the one who pulled her from her car and took her to the hospital, and that I was taking her place for Merry Mayhem since she can't be here. We got a lot of "ahhs" and "ooohs" for that.

There's no question that Josh is a fan-favorite going into this competition.

And I have a light-bulb moment. That's why Sam is here. He's sizing Josh up. Not because he's Violet's new boyfriend and Sam is jealous, but because Sam wants to win this contest and sees Josh as his number one opponent.

Well, he's right.

"Sam, this is Josh Evans," I say. "As you heard, he's a fire-fighter and paramedic. He does marathons and donates the prize money to animal shelters. And he's going to propose to Violet on Christmas."

What.

The.

Hell.

Did.

I.

Just.

Say?

Sam's eyebrows rise, and I hear Josh choke behind me.

"Uh, hey." Sam extends his hand to Josh. "I guess Nora left some of that out of your intro."

"Well, the proposal is a secret," Josh says easily, shaking Sam's hand, as if I didn't just stick both of my feet and one of his in my mouth. "So it'd be great if you didn't say anything to anyone."

I avoid looking at Josh.

Because I'm sure he's wondering what the *fuck*? And I have no idea how to explain it.

"Of course." Sam turns to Ashley. "And this is my fiancée, Ashley. Ash, this is Thea, Violet's sister."

"Yeah, I caught that," Ashley says, giving me a smile that actually seems genuine. "It's nice to meet you."

"Fiancée?" I ask. "Nora missed that part of *your* intro, too."

"Yeah, we just told our families this morning," Sam says, smiling down at Ashley. "She didn't want to tell the whole town from the stage in a big, public announcement. She wants to be sure friends and other family hear it from us first."

I narrow my eyes. I'm not 'other family' and I definitely do not consider myself a friend of his. "Well…great."

This is why I said Josh is Violet's fiancé. Because Sam does *not* get to come back to town after ripping up four years of her life and stomping on her heart and be all happy and at peace and… triumphant.

Okay, he might get to be happy and at peace. I'm not sure I can actually ruin that. But he will *not* be triumphant. Not on my watch.

"When are you getting married?" I ask them.

"Next summer," Ashley says, practically glowing.

"When do you think you and Violet will get married?" I ask Josh.

He looks at me with a *very* clear *what the fuck* look. I was right about that.

"We haven't talked about it," he says.

I'm sure that's true.

"She loves the spring. March maybe. Oh, March twentieth. First day of spring. Life feels fresh and new then, you know?" I look at Sam. "Throwing off the cold, old, dead shit and starting over? Love that. That's what we'll do."

Josh coughs. Sam actually takes a step back from me.

"That sounds…great for you all," he says.

The fucker is probably thinking how glad he is not to have me for a sister-in-law.

Yeah, he should be glad.

"So, we'll see you around this weekend, I guess," Sam says, taking Ashley's hand.

"For sure," I say. "A lot. Though you'll mostly see our backs." I laugh, but it sounds a little maniacal. I might need to work on that. "You know, because we'll be in front of you. Winning."

"Right." Sam smiles at me, then looks at Josh. "Good luck to you."

Josh gives a short laugh. "Thanks. You too."

I watch Sam turn and leave the stage.

Hey, did he wish Josh luck with Merry Mayhem, or was he wishing him luck dealing with *me*? That's what that sounded like.

Fucker.

Josh immediately turns to face me. "What the hell was *that*?"

"What?"

"Well, for one, I do not run marathons. I have donated money to animal shelters, but not prize money."

A twirl of warmth twists through my stomach. "You support animal shelters?"

"Of course."

"That's—"

"*Thea*, you have me marrying your sister in March!" he interrupts.

I nod. "You're welcome."

"I am *not* proposing to Violet on Christmas."

I wave that away. "Sam doesn't need to know that."

"What if he slips and says something to someone, and Bruce or Harley hears it? Or your mom?"

Yeah, that would be bad. I shake my head. "He won't. If he does, I'll tell them he's lying."

"It *is* lying."

"But that doesn't matter. I just did it to intimidate him."

"Why would that intimidate him?"

"He came over here to show us that he's perfectly happy and not at all worried about facing us in this competition."

"Did he?"

"Yes! He wants me to see him happy without Violet. He thinks that will get to me and I'll be flustered and not perform well."

"You do seem a little flustered."

"Well, now *he* can be flustered thinking about letting Violet go, and every challenge we win will just reiterate that you're the better man."

Josh shakes his head. "Thea, there's something I should probably—"

He's interrupted by Nora sliding in between us and grabbing my arm, "I don't know what to do." She's ditched the microphone and is now almost whispering.

"What do you mean? What happened?" I ask.

"Muriel and Patty are competing in Merry Mayhem!"

"Well…yeah, I know," I tell her. I gesture toward the now-empty chairs where the women had been sitting.

Her eyes are wide. "How? How are they going to do that? We have a *rock wall*…" She trails off. "Crap. I can't tell you that. You're a competitor. I can't tell you the challenges ahead of time." She drops my arm and looks around. "Where are Andi and Everly?"

"I need to talk to Andi too," I say quickly. "And you." I look up at Josh. "You're heading to Autre to get clothes and things, right?"

"If it's still okay that I come back here late?"

"Of course. It's fine." I take my phone out of my pocket. "Give me your number. We should have each other's anyway."

We exchanged numbers, and I text him my address and directions.

"I'll see you later then," he says. He hesitates as if he wants to say more, but then just says. "Okay. We'll talk later."

I nod. "Yep. Later. Drive carefully."

He leaves the stage, and I turn to watch him go. Once he's heading through the crowd toward Bruce and Harley's, I face Nora. "He's really hot, right?"

Her eyebrows climb. "Uh…yes."

"I mean, like anyone would think so. It's just a fact."

She nods. "Yes."

I puff out a breath. "Good."

"What is going on?"

"I needed to be sure that I'm attracted to him just because he's attractive, not because of...you know, anything more complicated."

She looks very interested now. "More complicated, like what?"

"He's *Violet's boyfriend*. So I can't be *attracted* to him. But I can find him attractive. That's different. You think he's attractive, too. So it's...fine."

"I do find him attractive. But that *is* different from being attracted to him."

I nod. She's confirming what I just said.

"So are you?" she asks.

"What?"

"Attracted to him?"

"I find him hot."

"Why?"

"Because he's sweet, and charming, and fun, and heroic, and..." I frown. "Why are you looking at me like that?"

"Because *I* find him attractive because of his blue eyes, his big biceps, and his nice ass."

My frown deepens. "I don't understand." Except, I think I do.

"Okay." She nods. For a few seconds. Then she says, "It will be okay. What's going to happen?"

"I could spend three days with him and like him even more in the end, and then have to watch him and my sister together when she comes home?" I groan. "Oh *God*, I'm horrible. She'll be coming home *from the hospital*. How am I even thinking this way?"

"Oh, come on, that's dramatic. You just met him, right? It can't be *that* much of an attraction," Nora says.

"I met him last June. He's the paramedic who was there with Harley."

"Oh."

I told Nora about Josh then. And that he visited Harley. And that they still text sometimes.

She agreed that he sounds amazing.

"Well…that's…a weird coincidence."

I sigh.

"So, you *are* attracted to him, but it's not…" She trails off, clearly not sure how to finish that.

I just look at her, lips pressed together. Then I confess, "This has *never* happened to me before."

Her eyes widen. "Oh."

"I hate it."

"Oh."

"We might need to pull out of Merry Mayhem."

Nora shakes her head. "Too late. Besides, you and Josh are the fan favorites. Right behind you are Sam and Ashley. If you pull out, they move into the lead."

"How do you even know that? We *just* did the kickoff."

"We polled people during the Get to Know the Contestants event," she says, as if that should have been obvious.

I roll my eyes. "So, my choices are spend all this time with Josh and just ignore my feelings, or let my sister's jackass ex win this contest that means so much to her? The one thing she did *not* want to happen?"

Nora nods. "Pretty much."

Great. My only shot at being a *good* sister is to spend the next three days in close proximity with her boyfriend, having fun, making merry, and being perfect partners so we can win this thing.

And trying really hard not to fall for him.

"Are you going to have the hot chocolate booth open all weekend?" I ask Nora.

"Of course."

"Be sure you keep the schnapps well stocked."

CHAPTER 10
JOSH

IT'S NEARLY eleven by the time I climb the steps to Thea's front door. The lights are still on in the front window, so I hope I won't wake her and Ruth.

I pause on the top step and take in the wreath on the front door, the lighted plastic gift boxes arranged by the front door, and the multi-colored lights strung along the gutter and the front railing. They're falling down on one corner, and I make a note to fix that in the morning.

And for the first time, I wonder where Ruth's dad is.

Not that Thea isn't capable of putting up and fixing Christmas lights on her house. But she's a single mom who owns her own business in her small hometown and clearly has a big family that she sees often. She's clearly doing a lot. How long has she been single? Is he around to help at all? Does he regret letting her go?

I only know the answer to one of those questions. That last one. He definitely regrets it.

Either that, or he's an idiot.

I pause at the door. Should I text and let her know that I'm here? She didn't give me a key, and I don't want to knock or ring the doorbell.

Josh: *I'm here. Front porch.*

I wait a few seconds, but get no answer.

I try the door. It's unlocked, which I don't love, but Rebel is small and she seems to know most of the town, so she knows better than I do if that's safe.

I still don't love it.

I push the door open and poke my head in. There's a small foyer with a pile of shoes on one side and several hooks on the wall full of jackets and sweaters. There's a staircase straight ahead, and light is spilling from a room ahead and to the right.

"Thea?" I call softly.

No answer. I step inside, shutting and *locking* the door behind me. I kick my boots off, adding them to the heap, and shrug out of my thick outer flannel, hanging it over the blue puffy jacket on the third hook.

I set my bag at the bottom of the staircase and take a deep breath. The house smells like cinnamon and caramel. Exactly like the caramel rolls my grandmother makes.

As if I didn't already have multiple reasons to want Thea Chabert.

I step into the living room. The TV is mounted on the wall facing me, and the movie playing isn't familiar but is clearly a Christmas movie. The actors are walking along a path with drifts of snow on either side, bundled up in coats, gloves, and hats. They're laughing as they pass park benches where people sit, sipping from paper cups, and there's a snowman in the distance. That looks a lot more like a Nebraska winter, than Louisiana.

The living room windows are to my right and are partially blocked by the Christmas tree, which glows with multi-colored lights, like the ones on the porch. The back of the sofa is directly in front of me, but I don't see Thea and Ruth.

Until I step around the end of the couch.

They're stretched out on the cushions under a big red fleece blanket with white snowflakes, facing the television, fast asleep.

My heart does a weird flip in my chest. That's such a sweet, peaceful sight and a thought flits through my mind. *Wish I could see this all the time.*

Followed immediately by *fuck, she's beautiful.*

Thea's face is devoid of makeup now, and she's pulled her hair back with a hairband.

I'm not sure what to do here. But I have to wake her up, don't I? All the lights are on, and I don't know which bedroom I'm supposed to use upstairs.

I lean over the back of the couch and brush a hand over her forehead. "Thea?" I say softly.

I drag the back of my fingers down the side of her face. Her skin is so soft. I want to run my thumb over her lips, but I resist. When I touch her lips, I want her awake.

"Thea?" I say again.

Her eyes flutter open, and she looks up at me.

"Hey, it's Josh."

Her eyes widen for a moment, then she blinks rapidly and looks around. "Oh, sorry. I didn't mean to fall asleep."

"No worries. I just got here."

She looks down at Ruth and then shifts, sliding her arm out from underneath her sleeping daughter. "What time is it?"

"Just after eleven," I say. "I'm sorry it's so late."

"It's fine." She pushes herself up, the blanket falling away from her shoulders.

She's wearing a soft-looking cotton T-shirt. And no bra.

It's not my fault for noticing. The evidence is right there. Two perky breasts, pressing against the front of thin, pale-yellow cotton.

She's clearly not aware of the eye full I'm getting, and I straighten as she sits up on the couch, shifting around Ruth in a maneuver that says she's done this many times before.

I'm grateful to see she's in long pajamas and socks. The pants are loose and tied at her waist, but they cover her legs, giving me less bare skin to become obsessed with. But they're also thin, and as she twists and bends, adjusting the pillow under Ruth's head and tucking the blanket around her, the pants cling to her hips and ass.

I admit to myself, however, that it wouldn't matter.

I'd be appreciating her shape no matter what she was wearing.

She and I definitely need to talk.

"Do you want me to help you get her upstairs?" I could easily carry Ruth up to her room.

Thea smiles down at her daughter. "I told her she could sleep on the couch by the Christmas tree tonight." She moves around the room, shutting off the other lights and the television, leaving only the glow from the tree illuminating the room. "Come on, I'll show you to your room."

I follow her out of the living room and grab my bag before climbing the stairs behind her, stubbornly keeping my eyes *off* of her ass in those pajama pants.

She probably thinks they're not appealing at all. She probably didn't even think of me when putting them on before curling up on the couch. If she did think about me showing up later, she probably thought washing off her makeup and dressing down would quell the flirtatious undertone and feeling of camaraderie we'd built tonight.

Maybe some men don't find blue, yellow, and white plaid sexy, but I find a woman in her element, completely relaxed and comfortable, and willing to let me see that side of her extremely hot. Anyone can look good with enough makeup, hair extensions, and other adornments. Being herself, in her own space, doing things her way is exactly how I want Thea.

"Since I don't know what time we might get a text in the morning, Ruth and I already showered tonight, so the bathroom is all yours tomorrow." She motions toward the door two doorways down. "Towels and stuff are in there. Help yourself."

"You think that we're going to have a surprise challenge tomorrow morning?"

"I saw the glint in Nora's eyes. I've seen that before. For sure, we're going to have a challenge before the scheduled one at ten a.m."

"Okay. I'll be ready."

She tips her head. "You're probably used to being called out at all hours. Your job isn't very predictable, is it?"

"That's for sure. I've always got my phone ringer on, and I can be up and ready to go in minutes, no matter what I'm doing."

She hesitates as if she wants to say something more. I would love it if it was something flirtatious and teasing about my ability to get ready to go.

Instead, she says, "I made some caramel pecan rolls for us to eat quickly if we have to leave in a rush. I hope that's okay."

I groan. "I'd hoped that's what I smelled. I could kiss you right now."

Her eyes widen slightly. "Probably not a great idea, everything considered."

"Everything considered?"

"My sister? Violet? You do remember her?"

I grin. "Of course." I have to come clean here. "I need to tell you something."

She shakes her head quickly. "No. You don't. I don't need details about you and Violet." She turns and starts down the hall toward, I assume, her bedroom.

"Violet and I are not dating."

Thea stops. Then turns back slowly. "Excuse me?"

I take a step towards her. "We're not dating. We barely know one another."

Thea frowns. "What are you talking about?"

I take another step. "I met Violet the night of her accident. That was the first time we ever talked. I agreed to come and do Merry Mayhem with her and pretend to be her boyfriend so that Sam didn't think she hadn't moved on after all these months."

Thea takes a moment, and I let that sink in.

Then she nods. "That makes more sense."

"It does?"

"Yeah. I've been annoyed that you're dating my sister because of Sierra. But if you're not really dating, that makes sense."

I take another step forward. "Hold on. What about Sierra?"

She hesitates. Then she crosses her arms. "I asked Ami about you. After we met, I found out you had visited Harley."

Ami, Amelia, is married to Michael, my Chief and one of my best friends. And, she is Ellie's granddaughter. That makes her Harley's great-grand niece. And some kind of cousin to Thea.

But I focus on my favorite part of what she said first. "You asked about me?"

"I did." She frowns. "And Ami told me that you followed a woman to Louisiana from Nebraska, changed your whole life for her, and were totally hung up on her, so I didn't go any further."

My heart thumps. I had no idea. Thea had asked about me and wanted to know more about me. "And what did you want to do?"

She shakes her head. "It doesn't matter. Ami said you were madly in love and not over Sierra."

"Ami was misinformed."

"Was she?" She looks completely skeptical.

"I *was* hung up on Sierra, yes. I did follow her here. That's all true. But she told me it was over. She moved on. I did too."

"Ami said you hadn't been with any other women."

Okay, well, there's that.

"I haven't," I admit. "But I..." I clear my throat. "I had plenty of that before."

"Plenty of 'that'?" Her brows are nearly to her hairline.

"Women."

"Ah. And before what?"

"Before I decided to get my shit together."

"What does that mean?"

I sigh. Okay, well, I want her to trust me, so I need to tell her everything. "I went job to job. Started and dropped out of school. Partied like hell. Drank. Slept around. And gambled. Hard. I did a lot of stupid stuff. I put my family through hell. My parents and brothers bailed me out more than once. My sister finally took a huge risk to get me out of a debt that I was going to get beaten for, fuck, maybe killed over." I shove a hand through my hair. "I had issues. But I got help. I started attending therapy. Gave up my 'friends', gambling, drinking, and women. And moved here to start over, and that helped a lot. Leaving all of that behind was the best move I could make. Sierra broke my heart, I'll admit. But that was over a year ago."

Thea hasn't uncrossed her arms, but she's not frowning anymore. "And Ami doesn't know that?"

"Ami's never asked me."

Thea chews her bottom lip. "But you wanted to spend time with Violet."

"No. Not…really. I mean, yes, I agreed to. The whole festival, competition thing, sounded fun. She seemed nice and needed a date. But we are not *dating*."

"What about the wedding… the accident…the ER…" Her eyes widen. "Did you *not* save Violet from the accident?"

"No. That's all true. I met Violet at Perks and Rec earlier that night. I actually came to town to visit Harley."

She looks surprised.

I shrug. "It was spontaneous. I was feeling restless. He was on my mind, so I just drove over and stopped at the house."

"Oh…wow."

"But he wasn't home. So I went to Perks and Rec to grab a burger. I was there when Chad, the guy she went to the wedding with, called. He was supposed to come to Merry Mayhem with her, and he was backing out. We got to talking and Violet asked if I'd be willing to step in as her partner, and I agreed."

Thea swallows. "So, you liked her."

"I…" I think back to that night. "We talked for, *maybe*, ten minutes. We weren't even flirting, Thea. I swear. We were talking about sucky Christmases, she told me about Sam, and then about Chad, and about Merry Mayhem. It was a very spontaneous deci-sion. I didn't *not* like her, but I wouldn't say that it was anything more than an interesting way to spend Christmas."

"You thought your Christmas was going to suck?"

I shrug. "My parents are concerned about me, and I'm the only single one in the inner circle over in Autre. I was going to feel…" I blow out a breath. "Lonely? Left out? Melancholy? I don't know."

"Because of Sierra."

"Because of what Sierra represented and what disappeared when she broke things off."

Thea's arms finally uncross. "What was that?"

"Being settled. A future. Someone to spend a Christmas with that we'd talk about thirty years later."

She takes a step closer, and I wonder if she realizes it.

"Is that what you want?" she asks.

I nod. "Yes."

"You seem really sure."

"Why does that surprise you?"

"You're…young."

I give her a half-smile. "Believe me, I enjoyed my youth. I did more stupid things before the age of twenty-three than a lot of people ever do. I'm good. I'm the baby of my family. My siblings are all settled and happy about it. My parents have been married for thirty-three years. Both sets of grandparents are happily married. In Autre, I'm surrounded by people who believe in happily ever after."

She knows the Landrys well. She knows what I mean. I see true love and loyalty every single day.

I study her in the dim light. The hallway is illuminated only by light from the bathroom, which appears to be a nightlight of some kind, and outside light filtering in through the bedroom windows on either side of the hall.

"So you're looking for something serious."

I nod. "Definitely. I mean, not with Violet," I say quickly. "That was just a spontaneous thing."

"It sounds like you're spontaneous a lot."

I chuckle. "Yeah. It's part of the package, I'll admit. I'm a thrill-seeker. It's how I ended up in a high-adrenaline job. It's how I ended up a gambling addict," I say, able to talk about it now where a few years ago, I'd deny it no matter who I was talking to. "I like a little chaos."

"That doesn't sound like someone who wants to settle down," she points out.

"Actually, settling down is *very* appealing. I want to be a paramedic and firefighter long-term. And I want to do things like take off on last-minute vacations, plan surprise parties, decide to take saxophone lessons, Christmas shop on December twenty-third, show up on my mom's porch without warning, decide that tonight is a great night to have pancakes for dinner…that kind of stuff. But I've realized that having a stable foundation, people I can really count on, a *home*, is hugely important to me being happy and being the best I can be."

She thinks about that. "Why didn't you just tell us about you and Violet from the beginning?"

"It was *her* plan. She wanted people to think she had a boyfriend. I don't know all the ins and outs of that. I felt like it was her secret and that I had to keep it until she was awake and could tell me how she wanted to go forward."

"Except with me."

"I needed you to know that we're not…"

She lifts a brow.

I decide to just go for it. "That we're not messing around behind Violet's back."

She doesn't say anything for a long moment. But she doesn't deny that something is happening here.

Finally, she takes a step closer to me. "And you really do like frosted sugar cookies, better than plain?"

"Without a doubt."

She presses her lips together, her eyes roaming over my face. Then she nods. "I do too."

"Wait, what? You like frosted sugar cookies better than plain?"

"Every single time."

"So, *you* lied." I grin.

"Yeah. Otherwise, we would've answered all five questions exactly the same, and I thought that seemed weird, since you are my sister's boyfriend. We shouldn't have *everything* in common."

I take the final step closer, which puts us toe-to-toe. "But I'm not your sister's boyfriend."

"No. You're not."

Heat is arching between us like I've never felt before. The hallway is hotter, and there is a humming in the air, almost as if someone has plugged in a generator.

"But we also haven't messed around behind Violet's back," she says softly.

"Right. I just—"

"Yet."

I stare at her. That one word takes a moment to sink in. Then satisfaction courses through me.

Yet.

"Yeah," I say, my voice gruff. "Yet."

"But…do you want to mess around? With me? Or do you want…more?"

Oh, fuck, I like this woman and how direct she is. "More, Thea," I say firmly. "Definitely more."

She pulls in a deep breath and tips her head back, looking up at the ceiling. "Dammit."

"Dammit?"

"I think knowing you're not her boyfriend and hearing you say that makes it worse."

"What? Why?"

She meets my gaze again. "Because the entire town still thinks you're Violet's boyfriend. My whole family does too. Violet thinks you're here at least pretending to be her boyfriend. If we act like there's something between us, we look like terrible people. My family is beloved in this town. My grandfather is the mayor. I have a business—"

"Wait, Bruce is the mayor?"

"No. Harley."

"Harley is the *mayor?"* But it only takes a moment to sink in and then, it doesn't surprise me.

"Yes. And I can't let people think I'm cheating on my sister with her boyfriend."

Fuck.

"And the town seems thrilled that Violet has a boyfriend," I say, thinking back to the *oohs,, aahs,* and applause we got when Nora explained who I am to the town during our introductions tonight.

"Correction, the town is thrilled that *you* are Violet's boyfriend. They think you're awesome, and they're thrilled that she has not only moved on but moved on with a great guy who Harley loves and who, once again, was a hero to my family."

"You sound like you're accusing me of something," I say, mildly amused.

"Well, if you were a loser, it might be easier for them to get over you, as well as being a cheater."

I chuckle. "If I were a loser, you wouldn't give me a second look."

"True."

"But you are giving me a second look, aren't you?"

"And a third," she says almost grudgingly.

I lift my hand and cup her cheek. "I don't want to date your sister, Thea."

"And I don't want people to think that we're cheating on her while she's in the *hospital.* I mean, at all, but especially with that."

I stroke my thumb along her jaw, loving touching her. Wanting more. "So we go out and do Merry Mayhem as friends, as Violet's sister and her boyfriend. Just as planned."

Thea nods. "We have to. We can't let on that we have any feelings."

I lean in. "But we do have feelings." I need to hear her say it.

I hear her breath catch, then she swallows. Finally, she whispers, "Yes."

Thank God.

"But, behind closed doors, when it's just us, I can do this." I brush my lips lightly over hers. It's not enough. And I don't want to stop there, but I know I have to take this slow.

"Have you ever kissed Violet?" she whispers against my mouth.

I pull back so she can see my eyes clearly. "No. Never. We've never touched."

"Thank God." She grabs the front of my shirt with both hands and pulls me close as she arches into me, pressing her lips fully against mine.

Or maybe I don't need to go slow.

My hands drop to her hips, and I turn her, backing her up against the hallway wall.

I don't intend to grind into her, but I lose all of my good intentions when her hands drop to my waist and she pulls me more firmly against her.

She moans as my hard spots seem to find all of her soft ones.

She's slender, but her hips fill my palms perfectly, and I itch to slide them around to her ass. Her breasts feel perfect against my chest, and I know I can sink into her for days.

It feels as if she's given herself permission to let go. As if she's been holding back, trying to control herself, and now she no longer has to.

Yes, sweetheart, let me have it all.

She's clearly intent on driving me out of my damn mind, because she lifts one leg and hooks it around my thigh, pulling me even closer.

Fuck it. My hands slide under her ass, and I lift her. With her back against the wall, her legs wrap around my waist, and now I can fit my hard cock against that sweet, warm space between her thighs.

We both moan now.

I rip my mouth away from hers. "Holy shit."

"I should say that I am shocked by this, but this is exactly what I thought it would be like," she says breathlessly.

I stare at her. "You've imagined this?"

"Yeah. When you answered Christmas Eve *and* Christmas morning. You can't wait for the good stuff, but you also like to drag it all out, right?"

It all makes sense to me. Maybe it wouldn't to someone else, but I understand exactly what she's saying.

And she's right.

"We had the same answer on that one," I remind her. And myself.

She catches her bottom lip between her teeth and nods.

I skim one hand up her side underneath the flimsy shirt she's wearing. She shivers at my touch.

"Is this something that we can pursue?" I ask her. My hand wraps around her rib cage, my thumb nestled under one breast. I revel in the way her breath saws in and out quickly and unevenly.

"What are you asking me? Birth control? How I feel about having a guy over with my kid at home? If I'm dating anyone?"

"Uh…yeah," I stammer. "All of that." I puff out a breath. "Fuck, I probably shouldn't admit that I forgot you have a kid downstairs."

She gives me a smile. "Never dated a single mom before?"

"Actually, no."

"It's particularly interesting when the child is old enough to move around the house on their own and understand some of the things they hear and see."

That stops my fingertips from stroking up and down the silky skin of her back. So she *has* dated.

"Oh."

She tightens her thighs around me. "I have an IUD. I've never had a guy here with my daughter at home. Or without my daughter at home," she adds with a little wrinkle between her brows. "And I'm not dating anyone." She pauses and studies my face again, then says, "I haven't dated in a really long time. I haven't had sex in a really long time either."

Heat licks through me, and I squeeze her side. "How long?"

"I'm really busy. And often really tired at bedtime. Let's just say that my vibrator, which can get me there in five minutes or less, is my favorite appliance. And I really, really like my espresso machine."

I take that all in and feel the corner of my mouth curl up in a very smug grin.

"Why are you smiling like that?" she asks, also smiling.

"Trying to decide what to say to that."

"Speechless?" she asks. "Never been with a woman who hasn't had sex in so long?"

"Not speechless," I correct. "Trying to decide if I should say that I can definitely get you off in under five minutes if that's what you need. Or if I should tell you that I absolutely promise every single five-minute increment you give me past that will be absolutely worth being a little tired in the morning."

She takes a deep shuddering breath, then shakes her head. "I'm also going to tell you that I've never been with a guy younger than me. You're gonna wear me out, aren't you?"

My laugh is louder now, and I press my lips together and glance toward the steps. Where her twelve-year-old daughter is sleeping. But I pin Thea with a very serious hot stare when I look back at her. "Yes," I say simply and firmly.

She just stares back.

"Tell me you're going to let me," I tell her, my voice husky, my hips pressing more firmly into hers, where I'm sure she can feel exactly the effect she has on me.

"Yes, Josh, I am going to let you."

Fuck, yes. I haven't felt this triumphant about anything in a really long time. Somehow, spending more time with this woman, having a chance to get close to her, having a chance to give her pleasure, and yes, being worthy of her giving me some of her precious time and sleep, feels like a huge accomplishment.

"But it's going to take a little juggling. Between Merry Mayhem and us not wanting anyone to catch on, and my daughter," she says.

I can see that she's a little sorry that I can't carry her down the hall to her bedroom right now.

"No worries," I tell her. I dip my head and take her mouth and a long, hot, slow kiss. Then I lift my head and let her slide down my body. Once her feet are on the floor, I step back and brush her hair away from her face. "Remember, I also like waiting till Christmas morning."

CHAPTER 11
THEA

I'M on my second cup of coffee by six the next morning.

Which sucks.

Not the coffee. I *love* my espresso machine, as I mentioned to Josh last night. But I've been awake since five. I'm not sure exactly when I fell asleep or when I woke up. I tossed and turned all night.

Because of Josh.

I'd been doing okay, telling myself he was off limits and that I was going to have to ignore my feelings. At least, I thought I was doing okay with that. I was *going to* do okay with that. Yesterday had been day one. I needed some time to practice ignoring my feelings.

Then he blew all of that up.

He and Violet aren't together.

He doesn't have feelings for her.

He has feelings for me.

Tingles race down my spine, and I gulp my coffee.

As if further revving my nervous system with caffeine is the answer.

But I definitely can't deal with all of this on five hours of restless sleep and no stimulants. Because today at Merry Mayhem, working right alongside him in front of the entire town—a town full of people who've known me all my life and know me very, very well—I'm going to have to act like I feel nothing for the big, hot, charming, sweet firefighter.

Who I feel a whole bunch of things for.

So you believe him?

The text is from Andi. I texted her and Nora about Josh. Because I can fully trust them to keep our secret, because I need to tell *someone*, and because there was a chance one or both of them was also already awake. Nora is for sure up. But she's, no doubt, running around getting ready for Merry Mayhem today.

Andi, on the other hand, keeps odd hours. She might have been up at three a.m. There was just as good a chance that she'd still be in bed at noon. But I took a chance.

Anderson Fleury is my best friend, besides Nora. Mostly because we're the same age—ie, older than the other women who hang out in our circle. I'm thirty-one, Andi is thirty-two. She ended up in Rebel because of her ex-husband. Before he was her ex. He left, and she stayed, thank God.

Andi and I don't have a lot in common besides our age and both living here, but we get along like long-lost cousins.

She's an artist. Literally. She mostly paints, but she also sculpts, does pottery, and even does some metal work, depending on her mood. She also teaches art classes for the Parks and Recreation department, and Nora hires her to create murals, signage, and other designs the department needs. It's sweet. Nora does it to give Andi jobs and, even more, to keep her from becoming a hermit in her little cottage outside of town. Because Andi has often expressed interest in becoming a swamp witch, and the idea of such isolation gives Nora hives. Andi knows this, which is why she agrees to the jobs even though she took her asshole ex's half of his very large bank account and investment portfolio, and she doesn't need the paycheck.

I've pulled Andi in on a few patient projects where I needed a brace or assistive device modified, but not to give her money.

It's because she's so freaking creative. With all of her tools and her ability to think outside the box, Andi was able to finagle things into workable adaptations, and the patients were delighted.

She has also painted a wheelchair and a walker for a pediatric patient, as well as two different wheelchair ramps. One went from a plain wooden contraption to a red-carpet entrance worthy of the little princess and her sparkly purple carriage, which Andi also helped create. The other became a colorful depiction of the older man's favorite sports teams. Both bring smiles to the people who use them every day. She even helped me redesign a patient's bathroom into something not only functional but much prettier when we were finished.

I've tried to talk her into going back to school for an Occupational Therapy degree, but she's very happy with things just as they are.

Now I think about her question. Do I believe Josh when he says that he and Violet are not dating? That they are actually nothing more than acquaintances, and just barely that?

Thea: *I do. It makes sense. If they'd been dating since that wedding, she definitely would have been talking about* Josh. *He's great.*

Andi: *That does make sense. Just be careful. Maybe he's just not into women in comas.*

I read her words and snort.

Thea: *Uh, if he WAS into women in comas, that would be a mark in the 'con' column, don't you think?*

Andi: *I'm going to say yes, being into unconscious women is a big 'con'.*

I roll my eyes. *Jesus, Andi.*

I realize deep down this is why I texted Andi. She's practical under her eccentricities. And more than a little grumpy. Especially when it comes to men.

That happens when your college sweetheart turns into a controlling asshole who then cheats on you and expects you to understand that it's your fault.

Okay, being happily single is also something we have in common.

Because I am. Happily single, that is. I haven't wanted or needed a man in my life in…ever.

Ruth's dad was a guy I'd started dating in college, and we ended up with a positive pregnancy test before we'd even met each other's parents.

He stuck around, helped me through the pregnancy, was there when Ruth was born, helped financially, still does, and sees her here and there, but I have full custody. He and his wife live in Houston. Ruth loves her two half-sisters, her dad, and her step-mom. It's, overall, a good situation for all of us.

And I've hardly done any of this on my own. My family, this whole town, has been there for Ruth and me, and they have helped in numerous ways.

But I haven't had a man in my life because…I haven't felt like I wanted or needed one.

And now Josh is here.

I know he's spontaneous and flawed, and also looking for something serious.

With me.

I had expected the bright daylight and caffeine, and the absence of his big hot body up against mine, to make all of that seem more ridiculous and to help me find a way to say no.

That isn't happening.

I hear the steps creak and my heart kicks against my ribs.

It's not Ruth. She's still asleep on the couch. Which means it can only be done by one person.

A moment later, Josh steps into the kitchen.

He's freshly showered and dressed in his boots, blue jeans, and a long-sleeved Henley.

His hair is still damp, and it appears he has just shaved.

God, he's cute.

He's young, too. He's five years younger than me. But he doesn't seem to care about our age difference.

Looking at him now, feeling my heart pound, feeling the tingles race along my nerve endings, I realize I don't either.

He's more mature than a lot of the twenty-six-year-olds I know. He's been through some stuff. Addiction, those consequences, and recovery. He also sees a lot as a paramedic and firefighter, I'm sure. He left his comfort zone and moved to a new place, a whole different world and culture in Louisiana from Nebraska. He realized he needed to change his life, and he did.

I don't think that five years between us matters.

Hell, he might be more mature than I am in a lot of ways. I've never lived more than sixty miles from home. I now live and work in the same town where I grew up. I'm definitely not what anyone would call spontaneous.

"'Mornin'," he greets, giving me a smile that slides over me like warm butter over a pecan caramel roll and makes my lower stomach clench.

God, I want to kiss him.

"Hi," I say. My voice sounds husky. "There's coffee. And the rolls are there on top of the oven."

"How did you sleep?" he asks, crossing to the coffee pot.

I don't even try not to check out his ass in those jeans. I might be attracted to him for more reasons than his blue eyes, big biceps, and nice ass, but I definitely noticed those as well.

"Not great to be honest," I tell him. "How about you?"

He turns and leans back against the counter, regarding me across the space of the kitchen. "Not great. I didn't think it would be appropriate to jerk off in Violet's bedroom. So, I slept most of the night hard and dreaming of you.",

My eyes widen. Okay. He talks blatantly about sex and has a little bit of a dirty mouth.

I don't hate it.

At all.

"Same. Kind of. Not the hard part."

One corner of his mouth turns up. "No vibrator use?" he asks.

"Because I'll be honest. Some of my sleeplessness was wondering what you were doing in your bedroom."

I lift my coffee cup to hide my smile, sip, and then set it back down. "I thought about it. But I didn't think it would be satisfying."

He nods as if what I'm saying is akin to discussing how much tinsel is appropriate on Christmas trees. "I love that you're already considering how much fun an extra ten or fifteen minutes could be."

I finally give up fighting it and laugh. "Oh, I didn't realize that was the offer. I guess my imagination ran away with me and thought it might be more like twenty or thirty minutes."

He walks toward me. He sets his coffee cup on the breakfast bar, then leans onto his forearms and pins me with a direct look. "Let me be clear. We're talking, you're gonna lose a couple of *hours* of sleep. Fair warning."

I lean over the bar and press my lips to his.

Yeah. The tingles from last night were not just a dark-hallway-late-hour thing.

He cups the back of my head and deepens the kiss.

I could definitely start every day like this.

Both of our phones ding at the same time.

I pull back, startled. I was totally lost in that kiss.

He just grins at me as he pulls his phone from his back pocket.

I look down.

It's from Nora.

It's Merry Mayhem Day One! Surprise Challenge One starts in thirty minutes! Town Square!

I look up at Josh. "Told you."

"Damn. Seven a.m. This is hardcore."

"You ready?"

His gaze drops to my mouth. "So ready."

I grin and push back from the breakfast bar so I can slide to the ground. "For Merry Mayhem."

He nods. "Yeah. Right. Merry Mayhem. That's what I meant."

I turn back in the kitchen doorway. "Remember, you're my *sister's* boyfriend."

His gaze lifts from my ass to my face. His eyes and tone are serious. "I am *not* your sister's boyfriend, Thea."

I feel warmth rush through me. "Remember, you're *acting like* you're my sister's boyfriend," I amend.

"Yeah," he nods. "For a couple of days."

"Right."

"*Only* for a couple of days," he repeats. "Don't make me resist you in public longer than that."

I'm smiling all the way upstairs, through getting ready, and the whole time he holds my hand on the drive downtown.

At two minutes to seven, Josh and I are standing at a long table in the town's square along with all of the other contestants. Before us are plates of plain sugar cookies, bowls of frosting, and multiple decorations—colored sugars, sprinkles, piping bags filled with more frosting in various colors, and tiny candy snowflakes, stockings, and candy canes.

We are also bundled together into one winter coat. We have our arms around one another inside the coat, and my left arm is in the left coat sleeve, Josh's right arm is through the right coat sleeve. I also have a mitten on my left hand, and he has one on his right.

All of the other pairs are in coats and mittens as well.

Muriel and Patty fought over who should get the right and who should get the left mitten. Jesse and Brad, the married couple, are just now putting on their coat and mittens because they have all their kids home for Christmas and couldn't get into the bathroom on time to get ready and get down here. The two teens, Mitchell and Max, were the first ones here and are directly across the table from us, grinning and seemingly excited about the contest. Sam and Ashley are cuddled up in their coat, whispering together, and smiling at each other like love-sick fools.

"If I'd known I'd get to be right up against you like this, I would have been *very* excited about this first challenge," Josh says, for my ears only. Beneath the coat, his left hand slides down to my ass.

"Behave," I tell him softly. But I really like his hand there.

Thank goodness it's only about fifty degrees this morning. It will be way too warm for a winter coat later. Not to mention being pressed up against this guy's hot body. Literally. He's *warm*.

"You're going to decorate as many cookies as you can in the next ten minutes, but you can each only use one hand. You need to work as a team!" Nora is grinning as if this is the most fun thing she's ever seen.

But Nora looks like that about every activity during Merry Mayhem.

Okay, she looks that way about almost everything the Parks and Rec department does.

"Whichever team has the most *well-decorated* cookies at the end wins. But there *will* be judging. The cookies need to look good, too."

"Really good!" a voice calls from the audience that has gathered to watch despite the early hour.

I look over and see Thurman Lafitte, otherwise known as Brewser. He's the retired town doctor, but was given the nickname long ago because, as a kid—the story varies between ten years old, six years old, and fourteen years old—he started helping an uncle brew beer and moonshine in their backyard. Considering that was sixty-some years ago, he's *very* good at it by now.

"You're one of the judges?" I ask.

"You know it!"

"And me!" His constant companion, William Bienvenu, whom they call Wilson because his bald head reminds them of a volley-ball in some Tom Hanks movie, is right beside him.

"Are they tough?" Josh asks.

I laugh. "Very. But they also like you a lot because you've been so good to Harley, and they're Harley's best friends."

"Harley has a lot of friends."

"He sure does."

"Does that mean we can get by with some sloppy cookies?"

"Maybe a couple of smudged edges, but nothing major."

"Okay then, let's go."

I grin up at him. "I'm ready."

He smiles down at me. "This is the most fun I've had in a *very* long time."

"We haven't even started," I protest with a laugh.

"I know."

Dang, it's really going to be hard to resist him in public for much longer, too.

"Ready, set, go!" Nora calls.

Jingle bells ring, and everyone reaches forward, the table bouncing as we bump into it.

"Grab the round one," I say. "We'll start easy with an ornament."

Josh grabs a round cookie and puts it in front of us.

"Are you right-handed?" I ask him.

"Yep. But pretty ambidextrous. I can start an IV with either hand. Can do sloppy sutures with my left if I *have* to. Can't intubate lefty though."

I stare at him.

"I mean, I can stabilize the tubing with my left, of course," he goes on. "I just can't thread the endotracheal tube with my left hand. Unless I *really* had to. I probably *could*." He seems to be thinking that over now.

I laugh. "Okay. I definitely think you should frost. I'll hold the cookie still."

Can the guy do *sutures* and intubate? Yeah, he can handle a piping bag.

He grins and grabs for the white icing, painting on a plain background, then reaches for the red piping bag.

Across from us, the brothers are bickering.

"I can't do it left-handed either!"

"Well, what are we going to do?"

"I don't know! Just do *something*!"

"I can't do shit with my right hand," one of the twins—I can't tell them apart—whispers to his brother.

"I can draw with my left hand, but I'm still shit. I'm a terrible artist," the other says.

"I've never used one of these things to decorate anything," the first twin says. "Can we just do sprinkles?"

"We can, but we won't get as many votes."

The twin who claims to be shit at drawing picks up one of the piping bags. "How does this work?"

I lean over. "Just squeeze from the top, like a tube of toothpaste. The frosting will come out the tip. Then just use it like a pencil."

The kid nods and puts the tip of the icing bag against the cookie. But he does it too hard. It digs into the frosting they've already spread on the cookie and drags that frosting with it.

"Not like that!" His brother protests.

"I don't know how to do this!" the one with the bag exclaims.

"Gentler," I say. "You're just writing on top of the other frosting."

I glance down at our cookie. And damn. Josh can do sutures, and he can draw a pretty great design with red frosting. It looks like basket weaving across the middle of our white round cookie.

I look up at him. "I'm impressed."

"My mom and aunt are great bakers. I might've had some practice in the kitchen growing up."

I grin. "How about silver balls across the top?"

"Awesome." He starts picking up the tiny balls between his thumb and index finger. He drops them into place in a perfectly straight line.

"You weren't kidding about your exceptional fine motor skills."

He shoots me a smirk and squeezes my ass at the same time. "I'm *very* good with my fingers."

I feel my cheeks flush as I look up at him quickly.

He winks. "Yes, that's exactly how I meant that."

"I don't know what you mean," I say breezily.

"Yes, you do. I can see exactly what you're thinking. And we are on the same page."

I drop my voice even lower. "Stop it."

"No one's watching us. Everyone's concentrating on their own cookies."

"We have an entire audience watching us."

"We just look like really good contest partners."

"Dammit!"

I look across the table to find the cookie that the twins were decorating crushed.

"This is hopeless," one of them groans.

They look so disappointed.

"We can't even get our *first* challenge right," one says.

"Maybe we should just back out," his brother says miserably.

"Oh damn," Josh groans as he drags the side of his mitten across his perfectly decorated cookie, smearing frosting and sending little silver balls rolling across the table. He looks at me. "Sorry. It's been a while since I did this."

I give him a little frown. It was obvious he did that on purpose. But I nod. Maybe we're teaching the guys a lesson. "It's okay. We'll just start over."

He looks across the table. "You have to be able to pivot quickly in something like this," Josh says. "Think on your feet. Get creative."

"Sure. But…we have to follow the rules," one twin says.

"But what are the rules *really*?" Josh asks.

"What do you mean?"

"You have to frost as many cookies as you can. And they have to look good, right? But "good" is in the eyes of the judges. We just need to impress them somehow," Josh points out. "That's it."

"What are you getting at?" I ask him.

Josh looks down. "Do you trust me?"

"Yes," I say honestly.

He grins. "Great." He looks across the table to the twins. "I have an idea. You up for trying something?"

"We have nothing to lose," one says, gesturing at the mess in front of them.

"Exactly," Josh says happily. "Start frosting the round cookies with white frosting. As quickly as you can." He looks at me. "Us too."

I laugh. "Okay."

"We're making snowballs," Josh says. "So they don't have to be perfectly round either." He pinches the edge of the cookie in front of him, making the edge jagged.

The boys are grinning, and I love the fact that he wanted to help the boys through this and turn their frustration into fun.

We quickly start frosting round cookies, completely white, and then, with Josh's instruction, dabbing the tops of them with multiple little white balls. The boys enjoy even crushing a few.

Then, as the timer ticks down, we scatter the cookies between us.

"Time!" Nora calls out happily.

Everyone steps away from the table, and we grin at the twins, who look like they've been let in on a big secret.

"Okay, judges, see what you think," Nora says.

Wilson, Brewser, and a couple of ladies from the city council start walking up and down the table. When they get to us, all eyebrows rise.

"This looks like you had a food fight," Brewser says.

"Kind of," one of the twins says. "Joint venture. The theme is snowball fight."

The crumbs in between us look very much like scattered snow, the round white cookies clearly represent snowballs, and we each have an "arsenal" piled up in front of us. All of the judges chuckle.

"Creative," Brewser says.

"I've never seen two teams work together to create something," one of the women, Susan, says.

I can't tell by the way she says it if that's a good thing or a bad thing.

They continue down the table, and we share a conspiratorial smile with the boys.

It doesn't really matter who gets these points. We had a good time. And I got to stand smashed up against Josh's side. I can think of worse ways to spend my early morning hours.

And better ways.

Like smashed up against Josh without all these clothes between us and without an audience.

Stop it. You're going to get in so much trouble.

After checking out all of the cookie decorating and huddling for a couple of minutes, the judges stand up and face us. "We're ready to award the points," they tell Nora.

"Excellent," she says, standing by the enormous whiteboard she'll be using to keep track of our scores over the next couple of days.

"This challenge was worth twenty-five points," Wilson says. "We have to admit that Jesse and Brad have the prettiest cookies decorated."

Jesse and Brad give little whoops and high-fives.

"*But,*" Brewser adds. "We are only giving them fifteen of the points. We want to give Thea and Josh five points and Max and Mitchell five points, too. We appreciated the teamwork and creativity."

Jesse and Brad are less happy now, but Max and Mitchell look like Brewser just told them they get to take all the cookies home with them, too.

"Um…" Nora stands with her whiteboard marker, poised. "I guess we never said all the points need to go to one team," she finally decides with a shrug. "Great!"

The audience applauds as Nora writes all the points on the board.

"Okay," she says, turning back. "The relay race starts at ten o'clock sharp. Grab some breakfast and coffee, and we'll see you back here. Well, at the statue," she says with a laugh.

The relay race will start at the statue of Julia the Otter. Of course.

The audience disperses to the booths that have been set up with breakfast foods, coffee, and, of course, the cocoa stand that is open throughout the event.

The participants in the cookie decorating contest shrug out of their coats and mittens and head off for refreshment as well.

I look up at Josh. "We could've kicked butt at that contest and gotten all the points," I tell him unnecessarily. "You're an excellent cookie decorator."

He sighs. "I should probably confess something to you as my teammate."

I think I know where this is going. "And what's that?"

"I'm not very competitive. I'm definitely a team player. And I like to help other people."

I put my hand on my chest and gasp. "No. The firefighter and paramedic is a helpful, nice guy who doesn't like to see other people struggle?"

He grins. "I'm going to struggle in the relay race and obstacle course against those two kids and the two older ladies."

I like him so much.

"Well…"

He turns to face me fully. "What?"

"The only real objective is for Sam and Ashley *not* to win."

Josh's eyes narrow, but his smile grows. "That's true. Are you thinking what I'm thinking?"

"That we can help everyone except them? That we could make sure that they don't win rather than worrying about winning ourselves?"

He nods. "Yes. I'm into that."

"Then I think you should know something," I tell him.

"What's that?"

"I really want to kiss you right now."

Heat flares in his eyes, and he takes a step closer. Too close. We cannot stand this close in public.

A point that is emphasized when Bruce and Harley come up behind me and say, "That was awesome."

I straighten and turn quickly to greet them with a smile that is probably too bright. "Thanks. We had a good time."

"You two are so good together," Amanda Long says enthusiastically. "It's so great that you get along so well since you're going to be in-laws."

I struggle to hold onto my smile.

They all think we're going to be *in-laws*. Josh is going to be my *brother-in-law*. Because he's with my *sister*. Ugh. "Well, Josh is pretty hard not to like."

Not a lie.

"You're jumpin' ahead there, Amanda," Harley says with a chuckle. "Violet and Josh are just datin'. Don't be scaring him off."

Amanda laughs and waves that away. "As if marrying into your family would scare someone off." She looks at us again. "Maybe the two of you need to keep being partners for Merry Mayhem in the future. Do you think your sister will let you borrow him?" she asks with a laugh.

Ugh times two. And yuck.

Of course, it's just me thinking of 'borrowing him' in dirty ways, I'm sure.

"Oh, I don't know," I say. "Josh is kind of the type of guy you wanna keep to yourself."

I hear him clear his throat behind me.

"Thea and I do work well together," he says. "This might just ruin Merry Mayhem for me in the future. This might be my first and last year."

"Oh, no!" Amanda reaches out and grabs his arm. "Violet loves this. She'll never want to give this up. She'll be so lucky to have such a great partner."

And just like someone dumped cold water over the top of me, I am reminded that not only is my sister missing out on one of her favorite parts of the year, but she's not here because she's hurt, in the *fucking hospital*. And everyone in this town thinks that I am here being an amazing sister to her, along with her amazing boyfriend, Josh.

We're doing this for her. Supposedly.

And that *is* how it started.

We've just…veered off course.

And next year, if Josh is here for Christmas, will it be with me? And if so, how will the town feel about us both then?

I wonder if they're serving spiked hot chocolate this early in the morning.

CHAPTER 12
JOSH

"OH GOD, THAT'S EGGNOG, RIGHT?" I ask.

"Yup," Thea confirms.

"Do we have to drink it?" I ask.

We're standing at the otter statue. The otter's name is Julia. But I know nothing else about it...her...the statue. I don't know why she's named Julia, and I don't know what she did to be deemed important enough to have a statue, commemorating her life in Rebel, Louisiana.

And now is not the time to ask. We are fifteen minutes away from the start of the relay race. The first big official event of Merry Mayhem.

And there are cartons of eggnog sitting on the table at the starting line.

"Honestly, it could go either way," Thea says. "Merry Mayhem is never the same year to year. There's usually a relay race, but the stations are different."

"So what can you tell me?"

I'm going in blind here. We have not been allowed to go check out the other stations and can really only see this first table, and I've never even been here as a spectator.

Thea shakes her head. "Even the number of stations varies

year to year. The rule is simply that we have to alternate. You do one, and then I do the next. The instructions will be at the station when you get there. You have to complete the task, but also do it quickly. So whoever reaches the finish line first, but has also completed all the tasks *correctly*, wins. If you miss a station or don't do the task right, you get deducted points."

I'm bouncing on the balls of my feet and feel like I should do a few jumping jacks. "Give me an example of a couple of tasks," I tell her.

"Okay, last year there was a station where we had to eat Christmas cookies, drink a glass of milk, and write a quick note to Santa."

I blew out a breath and roll my neck. "So physical and creative tasks."

Thea laughs. "Sure. I guess so."

I rub my hands together. My work is kind of the same. Yes, it's a lot of physical stuff. Still, sometimes you have to be creative in how you calm patients down, how you get their cooperation, how you fit yourself and equipment into tight spaces, how you make something work 'just for now' to stabilize them just long enough to get back to the ambulance or to the hospital.

"I'm definitely used to thinking on my feet," I tell Thea. "We want to be quick, but also careful. That's what I do every day."

She giggles.

The sound is so surprising, I look down at her. I want to kiss her. That thought hits me like someone smacked me across the face.

"Get your game face on, girl," I say with a little growl.

She shakes her head. "This is just for fun. It's not life or death. Take it down a notch."

I turn to face her. "I'm either on or off. I give my *all* to everything I do."

Her cheeks get a little pink, and I feel a surge of satisfaction for taking her mind exactly in the direction I intended.

I will *definitely* give my all to any activity she agrees to with me behind closed doors. She wants multiple orgasms in a variety of positions? I'll deliver. She wants me to cook her dinner? It will be the best thing she's ever eaten. She wants a movie marathon? I'll movie-marathon the hell out of her.

She swallows hard. "I thought we agreed that it was more important that Sam and Ashley not win than that we win."

I glance to my left, where all the rest of the contestants are lined up waiting. "Right. True."

"So here's what I'm thinking," she tells me. "Jesse, Brad, Beckett, Sutton, and Max and Mitchell will be fine. Physically, they'll be able to do all the tasks, and they've all been observers or participants before. They're also all from here, so if there's any Rebel trivia—"

"There might be Rebel trivia?" I ask.

She nods. "There has been before. Or things like matching holiday recipes with who submitted them."

My eyes widened. "I don't know anyone in this town. I can't do that!"

"That's what I'm saying!" Thea exclaims with a grin.

"So what's your plan?"

"Muriel and Patty have lived in this town all their lives. They are a part of nearly every planning committee in this town, and they know every single person."

I'm nodding. Got it. Muriel and Patty are going to crush any trivia or matching games.

"Ashley is not even from here, and Sam definitely leaned on Violet for that stuff. But Sam and Ashley have a physical advantage over Muriel and Patty."

"So Muriel and Patty *should* win this one, but they'll struggle with the physical stuff."

"Right. The thing about this relay is that it's got multiple levels. If someone's *not* good at trivia, they might be really good at the physical stuff."

"The perfect team would have both..." Her meaning dawns. "You're going to ditch me?"

She shrugs. "It's for the greater good."

I clutch my chest. "I'm devastated."

She grins. "No, you're not."

I'm not. This is actually fun. Those ladies will need a little help and, hell, so will I. Not that Thea won't know the trivia answers, but I can't try to beat two old ladies. I just can't. I'd end up carrying one on my back and one in my arms across the finish line anyway.

I lean in. "Is this for the rest of Merry Mayhem or just for this event?"

"Well, there's a scavenger hunt and an obstacle course planned in the next few days," Thea says. "No way can Muriel or Patty do a rock wall."

Yes, I remember how Nora slipped with that little detail, too. "And I'm guessing these ladies will absolutely know the best houses for scavenger hunt items."

"For sure," Thea agrees.

She probably will, too, but maybe Sam and Ashley won't.

I haven't looked at the list of activities. I don't know what else is ahead. I've been way too wrapped up in this woman and just being here. But I love that she doesn't want Muriel and Patty to struggle with the activities.

I slowly nod. "Fine. Let's go find our new teammates."

Thea smiles as if I just told her she's won a year's supply of frosted sugar cookies, and I realize I'm a goner. The woman could ask me to drink two gallons of eggnog, and I'd ask if she wanted me to also eat some figgy pudding. I don't even know what that is, but I don't want to.

"Muriel, Patty, this is Josh Evans," Thea introduces me a minute later.

Patty pulls her cherry red sunglasses off her nose and nods. "Hello, Josh."

She is a beautiful and sophisticated-looking older woman with deep smile lines around her mouth and eyes, and snow white hair that is curled in perfect waves away from her face. She's wearing bright red lipstick that matches the sunglasses and the silk scarf around her neck. She's otherwise dressed in all white, from the thin sweater to the wide-legged pants to the boots on her feet.

Interesting choice for an outdoor activity.

"Nice to meet you," I tell her.

"You ever find those big shoulders are a problem?" Muriel, the woman to Patty's left, asks.

Muriel looks much like her twin sister, of course, but Muriel is…more. On top of her bright white hair, she's wearing a multi-colored turban. She's got on grape-purple eyeglasses that dwarf her face. She's dressed in a long tunic in a multitude of colors— more purple, along with turquoise, hot pink, and orange—and black pants. Overall, she's got on a pink fur coat.

"I um…" Her question throws me off. "In what way?"

"What kind of question is that?" Patty scolds.

"What? I'm just curious," Muriel asks. "You want me to start with if he likes cat or dogs more?"

"You don't need to ask him anything!" Patty says.

"Why can't I ask him things? We're human beings. We are supposed to talk to one another. And I'm an old woman. I don't know how much time I've got left, so I feel like I should start with questions I actually want the answers to. I don't care if he likes cats or dogs, but I'm curious if having wide shoulders and big arms like those gets in the way. When Russel and I would make out in the car, his wide shoulders were a hindrance to him reaching my—"

"Stop it," Patty snaps.

"My *zipper*," Muriel says. Then she shoots me a sly smile that says she didn't mean zipper at all.

"I um…" Then I nod. "There have been two times when I needed to get into a car to rescue a victim, and I needed another paramedic to do it instead because my shoulders were too big to fit in the space."

Muriel looks triumphant. "Exactly. You need lots of space to do your best work."

Is that an innuendo? I look at Thea quickly. She doesn't look shocked at all. I can only assume that it *is* an innuendo, and that's not unusual for Muriel.

"My Russel had wide shoulders, and we got a big old SUV to accommodate."

"Russel was your third husband, wasn't he?" Thea asks. "You were married to him…later on."

"What's your point?" Muriel asks her.

"That maybe some of Russel's trouble with reaching…everything…when you were making out in a car was that you were both old and not as flexible," Patty interjects.

Oh my God.

"Well, I did start wearing more muumuus," Muriel says. "That wasn't just because I don't like waistbands. You can go without panties pretty easily under a muumuu, and hiking it up is—"

"Stop trying to be shocking," Patty interrupts. "These two came over to chat."

"I'm trying to be *helpful*," Muriel says. "Old people are supposed to share wisdom with younger people." She squints at Thea. "You remember what I said about muumuus, okay?"

Thea nods. "I'm afraid I won't be able to *stop* thinking about it, Muriel."

Muriel chuckles.

I have to admit that I'm now picturing Thea in a muumuu with it hiked up around her waist, too.

"So, we actually came over with a proposition," Thea says. "What would you two say about switching partners?"

Muriel slides up next to me and hooks her arm through mine. "Sure."

Thea presses her lips together, clearly fighting a smile, but then she explains our thought process and the rest of the Merry Mayhem activities, leaving out only the part where we don't want Sam and Ashley to win.

"We'll be unbeatable," Muriel tells me.

I grin. "Can't wait."

We go to Nora, tell her we want to switch our teams, and point out that there are no rules that prevent us from doing so. She loves the idea that this will allow Muriel and Patty to fully participate in the activities she was concerned about. She calls the judges over, and they all agree.

"What about the points Josh and Thea earned during the first challenge?" Wilson asks.

"We'll split them between their new teams," another judge suggests.

Thea and I nod. "That's fine with us," she says.

Sam and Ashley still have zero points. That's all that matters.

"Okay, that's done," Nora says. "Everybody up to the starting line."

"Muriel, how do you feel about eggnog?" I ask as we all take our positions. When the jingle bells jingle, the member of the team who will do the task at station one will stay, while the other runs on to station two, twenty feet down Main Street.

"I've had way worse things in my mouth," Muriel tells me.

I laugh. "Then you're up first."

"You *haven't* had worse things in your mouth?" she asks, getting into position at the starting line. She only has to go about five feet to the first table.

"Maybe kale," I say. "But I can't think of much else."

"You're young," she says. "Promise me you'll put more things in your mouth before you're my age."

I laugh. "I'm not sure that's solid advice, Muriel."

"Just don't be the kind of guy who only sticks with what he knows or assumes that the things he likes are the epitome. I can assure you that you'll taste more good things than bad if you take chances on new things. And I'm old. So, you have to listen to me."

"What about poisonous things or things that might make me sick?" I tease.

Her eyes widen. "Well, don't eat poisonous things, Josh. Lord, do us old people have to tell you *everything*? I figured that was a given."

I laugh even louder. "Got it. Put more *edible* things in my mouth."

She gets a sly grin on her face. "Well, not necessarily *edible*. But nothing *dangerous*."

"What do you—" I catch on a second before completing the question. "Muriel!" I say, acting scandalized. I'm actually beyond amused.

"My first husband did not like…that…in his mouth. My second thought that he did, but he didn't really *appreciate* it. My third…" She sighs. "I still miss that man."

"Wide-shouldered Russel?" I ask.

"Yep. I only got seven years with him. But he had *years* to figure things out before I came along. Most things in life just take practice, Josh. Being a good firefighter, being a good friend, being good in bed…you just have to want to be good, and then you have to do it. Over and over again until it's second nature."

I nod. "Got it."

"Now let's kick some ass at this relay race."

We high-five just as the bells ring.

Muriel gulps her cup of eggnog like a champ.

Ashley gags on hers, which I sympathize with.

But Patty swallows hers no problem.

At the next station, I throw all three of my snowballs—made with a snow cone machine—and hit the bullseye on the target with two of them.

Sam only hit one bullseye.

But Thea hits all three.

My long legs are the only thing that puts me a few steps ahead of her.

Muriel wraps the odd-shaped baseball bat like a pro at station three, but so does Patty. Ashley struggles. She covers her poor paper wrapping with extra bows. Interestingly, Max pulls ahead at that station, wrapping the bat perfectly and pulling ahead of Muriel and Patty, getting to station four.

At station four, I dress the stuffed otter in the provided reindeer costume, including antlers, a Santa jacket, and little red and white booties, faster than Thea or Mitchell.

Sam and Thea finish at the same time I do, and again, I'm just slightly faster, getting to station five only two steps ahead of Thea. Mitchell beats us both by a step.

Thank God, Muriel is up on station five, where she has to play "We Wish You A Merry Christmas" on a xylophone. I never would have been able to pull that off. It seems that Muriel is the musical of the twins, because Patty hits a few sour notes. Ashley doesn't even know where to start. She simply clinks random keys. Max is perfect note-wise, but not as fast as Muriel.

We're barely ahead as Muriel sprint-walks to station six.

It's the last station, and I'm ready. I pull three small gifts out of a stocking and have to unwrap them. That's all fine. But then I have to figure out which judge each gift goes to.

Considering I don't know these people at all, I'm stuck.

Every stocking has different gifts inside, so I can't even watch the other participants.

I'm holding a lipstick—there are three female judges, and all are wearing lipstick this morning. I've also got a pack of double A batteries and a fancy chocolate bar.

A chocolate bar? Couldn't that go to anyone? And batteries? Everyone in the world needs double-A batteries.

So, I guess.

I hand the lipstick to one of the women, the batteries go to Brewser. Just as I'm headed for Wilson with the chocolate bar, Mitchell comes up next to me and whispers, "Sally. The one in yellow."

Then he's off, distributing his gifts. But I decide to trust him and hand the chocolate to the woman in the yellow cardigan.

And that was the right match. I was also right about the batteries. Well, actually, it turns out that the gift would have been right no matter who I gave it to. In a fun twist, every team had one gift like that.

But my lipstick choice is wrong, and Thea, Mitchell, and Jesse have already distributed their gifts before I'm finished anyway.

Thea and Patty win.

Max and Mitchell are in second place, and Beckett and Sutton —whom I wasn't even paying attention to—are third.

"We'll kick their butts at the ornament hunt," Muriel tells me.

"The what?"

"The next challenge," she says. "It's like an Easter egg hunt, but they'll hide Christmas tree ornaments around the park. Whoever gathers the most wins."

I grin. "Sounds good. See you this afternoon."

"See ya."

"Sorry about that," Thea says from beside me as we watch Patty and Muriel walk away, already bickering about how Patty should have definitely been able to play that song on the xylophone and how Patty hasn't played a xylophone in forty years, so how was she supposed to do that, and how neither has Muriel, but she did it.

"Don't be," I say. "Muriel's great."

Thea lifts a brow. "Now I *know* you're too good a guy to be real."

I move closer to her. "I'm *very* real, Thea. Want me to prove it?"

She takes a deep breath. "Yes."

I lean in.

But she steps back. "But you can't."

Right.

Fuck.

This shouldn't be so hard to remember.

"Come on!" Bruce calls us. "Lunch at our place!"

Thea looks relieved.

"You don't have to seem so happy not to be alone with me," I say with a chuckle.

"We just can't be late for the next challenge," she says as she starts walking.

"Would we be?" I ask.

She looks back over her shoulder. "Oh, yes."

Two and a half more days. I just have to *not* grab her and kiss her in front of this entire town for two and a half more days.

They're going to be the longest of my life.

Lunch is nearly as chaotic as everything else has been today.

Bruce has a buffet of sandwich fixings, a few sides like chips, pasta salad, and fruit, along with various Christmas treats— fudge, cookies, and chocolate-dipped pretzels—laid out. But he and Harley are getting ready to leave.

Bebe and Eli have returned from visiting Violet at the hospital. Now Harley and Bruce are going to sit with her.

I feel a stab of guilt as they fill us in on the doctor's report.

"She's doing great. They're going to wake her up soon," Bebe says with a wide smile. "All of her vitals are strong and stable."

That's great to hear, of course. I knew she'd be fine, but it's great to hear her progress. But I have to force a little extra enthusiasm into my tone. "That's amazing," I say. "I'll go up later after the ornament hunt."

I have to, right?

"Oh no, you need to stay here," Bebe says. "They might have a surprise challenge."

"Another?" I ask. "We just did one this morning."

Bebe and Bruce both nod. "You never know. You really should stay just in case."

I look at Thea. She looks confused, too. "There's never more than one surprise challenge a day," she says.

"Oh, sure. They did that three years ago," Bruce says, looking to Harley for confirmation.

He nods. "Something like that. It's definitely happened before. The scoring is close. And now you've got Muriel and Patty as partners. You need to be here for them."

Thea and I exchange a look. She shrugs. "That's true. We can't leave them without their partners." She looks at her mom. "I feel bad that I haven't been up there, though."

"Why?" Bebe says. "Violet's exactly where she needs to be. She might need your help once she's home, but there's nothing you can do at the hospital. She's doing fine."

"I guess," Thea says with hesitation.

"We're going now," Harley says, heading toward the door with his cane. Bruce is right behind him.

At the door, they have to step back to let Andi in. "Hey, guys," she greets, giving them each a hug. "Heading to New Orleans?"

"Yep. You need anything?" Bruce asks.

"I'll text you if I think of anything," she says. She shuts the door behind them, then joins us in the kitchen. "Hey, what's up?"

"We need your help," Thea tells her.

Clearly, Thea texted Andi to join us.

"Hit me." Andi starts loading a plate at the buffet.

"I need two methods of transportation for Muriel and Patty tomorrow during the obstacle course," Thea says, sitting at the dining room table with her lunch. "Light weight, easily maneuvered for me and Josh, but sturdy enough to carry them between stations over grass and gravel."

"Mom!" Ruth suddenly runs into the room. There's another girl her age with her. "Jordyn wants Anna and me to spend the night tonight. Can I?"

"Your mom is okay with it?" Thea asks the girl.

"Completely. You can text her."

"I will later. But yes, it's okay with me. Go home and grab your stuff. Take the pan of pecan rolls out of the freezer and take them with you. That way Steph won't have to feed you in the morning," Thea says.

I make a little noise of protest. She's giving pecan rolls away?

Thea clearly hears me and shoots me a grin. "I have something else for you."

God, I love that grin. I love her flirty. I want whatever she has in mind for me. *Whatever* she has in mind.

"Thanks!" Ruth and Jordyn call out as they run from the house.

"You need to get Muriel and Patty around the obstacle course quickly and easily," Andi says, picking right up on the conversation as she takes the seat perpendicular to Thea's.

"Yeah." Thea picks up a chip and pops it into her mouth. "I was thinking…the rules don't say that pairs have to take turns on the obstacles. They both have to be there and "participate". I'm thinking if Josh and I can get them around the course with us and we have them do the things they can, we take care of everything else, we can't be disqualified."

"Well, disqualifying people for being physically unable to complete a task would be very shitty and probably even illegal… Nora would never do something like that," Andi says. "If you all try to make accommodations and help them participate as much as they can, Nora will love it."

Thea nods. "Agreed. What do you think?"

"I can just put Muriel on my back," I say. "Piggyback."

Thea and Andi both laugh.

"Okay, that would be worth seeing. If we can't come up with something else, good to know that's an option," Andi says.

"Well, *I* can't do that with Patty," Thea says, with a grin.

"I can finagle something," Andi says. "Is the course at the high school like usual?"

"Yes, on the football field, so it's not too uneven or anything. There's grass, gravel, sand…oh, and blacktop, some pavement. Maybe a few cracks there."

"Got it."

I look from Thea to Andi and back to Thea. "She's just going to make something?"

Thea sips from her sweet tea. "She's going to find something and modify it as needed."

"Something like what?"

"First thing that comes to mind is a golf cart, but I think that's too big," Andi says.

"Yeah, it needs to be able to get in close to the stations so they can do as much as they're able," Thea agrees. "It might also be considered cheating if it's motorized."

"True. I guess that rules out Segways, too," Andi says with a grin.

Thea laughs. "Muriel would be a menace on a Segway."

"No way would either of them agree to use a wheelchair," Andi muses.

"Nope."

"I don't think they could get in and out of a red wagon easily," Andi says.

Thea shakes her head. "Or fast enough. Patty has had a hip replacement, so that wouldn't be a good idea anyway."

Andi shrugs. "I'll figure something out."

Bebe and Eli settle at the table, and we chat and eat. The time flying, until suddenly the alarms on our phones go off and we realize our next challenge is thirty minutes away.

Everyone rises and starts cleaning up, but I snag Thea's shirt and tug her out of the kitchen.

"Is something wrong?" she asks as I pull her into the alcove by the front door.

"Yeah. I haven't had a minute alone with you where I can do this." I cup the back of her head and kiss her.

She melts into me and lets me kiss her for nearly a full minute. I run my hand down her back to her ass and squeeze as I press her into the wall.

I give a low groan as she arches against me, letting me feel her curves through the thin sweater and skinny jeans.

I glide my palm over her hip and then up to cup her breast. She moans, but then pushes me back. She stares up at me with dilated pupils, her hands just resting on my chest.

"We can't do that unless we're behind closed doors," she says.

"Well, unless we're out of sight," I say.

She shakes her head, pressing her lips together for a moment, making me wonder if they're tingling a little. Like mine are.

"This makes it harder not to look at you with all my feelings on my face."

I smile. "I suppose you think I should be sorry about that."

She shakes her head, but she's smiling too. "I'm so glad to hear Violet is getting better. I want this all out in the open, too."

"Definitely." I run my fingers over her cheek, then drop my hand and step back. "Okay, I'll be good. I've just wanted to kiss you, well, ever since I last did."

She nods. "Me too. What are we going to tell everyone?"

"The truth. As soon as Violet is awake and everyone can see she's fine and she can agree that she and I just set this up last minute, for fun, but that it's nothing serious, then we can tell them how I was going to help her out but fell for you instead."

"Fell for me?" she repeats softly.

"Completely," I say firmly.

She takes a deep breath. "Yeah, okay. I like that. We'll tell them just what happened. The truth about you and Violet."

"And you."

"And me."

"Exactly."

"Thea! You ready to go?" her mom calls.

Thea stretches up and presses her lips to mine quickly. Then she calls back, "Yep. Totally ready!" She gives me a sweet smile, then ducks around me. "By the way, I'm sorry."

"For what?" I ask, realizing I need to go to the bathroom or something to explain why she and I were both out of the kitchen.

"For me and Patty totally kicking your and Muriel's butts in the next several events."

I chuckle. "You're going to have Andi put something amazing together for you and some rickety old thing for me and Muriel?"

She laughs. "Good idea."

Then she winks at me, and I barely resist reaching out and pulling her back into this little corner with me.

Soon. Soon we can come clean.

CHAPTER 13
THEA

"I LOVE THIS SO MUCH," Nora says, her eyes a little watery as she faces the town. "We have a five-way tie!"

We all smile at each other. Five of the pairs ended up with the same number of ornaments from the hunt in the park. But not accidentally. We all helped each other to find ornaments.

It started with Beckett realizing that the first two ornaments he found were hand-painted by Andi.

Patty confirmed that Andi's art classes had painted all of the ornaments in the park.

Beckett is a big fan of Andi. Not just her art, but all of her.

It's too bad for him that Andi has sworn off all dating, all men —especially younger, sunshiny, golden retriever hockey players— and even all flirting.

Still, Beckett decided he wanted to collect as many of Andi's hand-painted ornaments as possible, so he made a deal to exchange any other ornaments he found with Andi ornaments that other people found.

That led to Jesse making the same deal, but for ornaments that her kids had painted in the classes they take with Andi.

Muriel then decided she wanted to collect all of the ornaments *she* had painted and agreed to do the ornament exchange with anyone who found those.

We all ended up in the middle of the park, looking over all of the ornaments and swapping back and forth until everyone had what they wanted.

And an equal number of ornaments because, at that point, that only seemed fair.

But, as Beckett pointed out when one of the judges came over to see what we were doing, there are no rules against trading ornaments or a tie.

It would have been a six-way tie, except Sam and Ashley never came over to see what the ten of us were laughing and conspiring about.

"I'm really proud of you," Patty tells Muriel as the rest of the contestants begin to disperse.

Technically, we don't have anything else scheduled until tomorrow morning. There are, of course, plenty of food and craft booths to peruse, treats to sample, and holiday decorations to enjoy, though if people are feeling festive.

"Why?" Muriel asks.

"You were really nice and cooperative during the ornament hunt, you didn't insult anyone else's ornaments, and you didn't piss anyone off."

Muriel just shrugs. "You're the only one I like pissing off."

"You like pissing lots of people off," Patty argues.

"Okay, but you're the only one I piss off *on purpose*," Muriel corrects.

"But you admit you still like it when you piss people off besides me."

"Nine out of ten times," Muriel agrees.

Josh chuckles, and we exchange a look.

The easy way he gets along with the often-cantankerous Muriel is just one more thing I like about him. He seems to roll with whatever and whoever crosses his path. I'm sure that serves him well in his line of work, but it also makes him a very good fit for Rebel. We're an…eclectic bunch.

He suddenly stretches and yawns. "Man, it's been a big day."

"There might be something else yet tonight," Muriel warns him. "Don't you be fallin' asleep and missing a notification."

He nods. "No worries. I've always got my phone on. But I might need a nap." Again, he catches my gaze.

Suddenly, nap has a whole new meaning in my life.

And I need one too. Badly.

"It's been so busy, I've got some paperwork and laundry to try to get done," I say with a nod. "I'll probably head back to my house and hope we don't get a surprise challenge."

Muriel shakes her finger at me. "You'd better keep your phone on, too."

"Of course."

But I'm seriously considering bribing my cousin not to surprise us with any challenges for at least an hour. Or two.

Without a word about a specific plan or a "want to come to my place?", Josh and I start walking toward my house together.

We don't talk. We also don't stop, even when people call out to us with "Hey, Josh! Hey Thea!" or "You guys were great today!" We just lift our hands and give a quick, "Hi" and "Thanks!"

We climb the porch steps together seven minutes later, and I open the door.

What should I say? Should I invite him to my room? Should I just start taking my clothes off? Should I turn and push him up against the door and kiss him? Because I *really* want to kiss him, and I want him to know that. I also want him upstairs in my bedroom. Right now.

He steps in behind me and shuts the door. He locks it, then turns to face me.

I tuck my bottom lip between my teeth and wait.

Say something dirty and amazing. Tell me what you want. Tell me what to do. It's been a really long time and…

"I'm crazy about you, Danger," he says, his voice gruff.

That wasn't what I was expecting. I was expecting something dirty and demanding, or maybe funny and flirty. But that was just straightforward and sweet.

So, I give it right back to him. "I think you are an amazing man, and I am so glad that you want to be here with me."

He takes two steps forward and cups my face with both hands.

"I am so fucking glad that every other man who has ever been in your orbit was too damn stupid to see what was right in front of him. I am so glad you're not taken."

My heart starts thumping harder. "I am too," I tell him honestly. "I'm glad you finally showed up."

He gives me a grin and strokes his thumbs along my jaw on both sides. "Sorry it took me a little bit."

"I think it'll be worth the wait."

Heat flares in his eyes, and his smile fades into a hot, hungry look. "Oh, I can guarantee it."

He lowers his head, but I'm already arching to meet him partway.

Our mouths collide, and I feel an equal mix of lust and relief.

I've been wanting this all day.

Maybe all my life.

He seems to feel the same. His hands drop to my waist, and he pulls me more firmly against him as he deepens the kiss. I thread my fingers into his hair and hold him close as I try to show him that I am all in here. I want everything.

It's going to be complicated and messy to explain this to everyone, but I'm going to worry about that later.

It's not like this is the first time I've done something messy and my family stood beside me. This whole town did. I have to believe they'll be happy for us. And they'll believe us when we tell them what's really going on.

He kisses along my jaw to my ear. "This is your chance to tell me I still have to wait, that it's too soon, that...whatever. But take that chance quickly. Because I want to strip you down, spread you out, and make you scream."

Oh, God. I want all of that.

"I don't want to wait." I feel like I've *been* waiting. It's too… romantic, or something, to think I've been waiting for Josh specifically. That doesn't happen, does it? The soulmate thing? The there's-only-one-guy-who's-perfect-for-me thing can't be real. But I have never felt so sure of someone before.

He takes a long breath in. "If I get you naked, you're not getting dressed again until tomorrow morning, and I'm spending the night in your bed, Thea."

"I know."

There's a rumble in his chest, and then I'm being swept up and tossed over his shoulder.

I laugh and just hang on.

"You knew that was coming, right?" he asks as he starts up the stairs.

"I didn't know, but I hoped. You know the firefighter thing is really hot."

He smacks my ass and I gasp, then giggle.

"It does come in handy at times."

In the upstairs hallway, he stops before making it to my room. He lets me slide down his body and then presses me against the wall.

"I need to start right here. Right where we were last night."

Oh, I like that.

"I've had some very nice fantasies about how things went in this hallway if I were not as willing to be such a nice guy," he says.

I grin up at him. "You are absolutely incapable of not being a good guy."

"I said nice. Not that I wouldn't be *good*."

The word good carries a lot of sexy meaning.

"Part of me wants to tell you to go put on those pajama pants that I'm obsessed with," he goes on. "But I don't want to wait even another second."

He slips his hands under the bottom of my shirt and then strips it up over my head. I happily raised my arms to help.

He takes me in, leaning against the hall wall, in my emerald green bra and blue jeans.

"Anything you don't want to do, anytime you want to slow down, anytime you want me to stop, you just say the word," he says.

I nod.

His gaze is intent on my face. "I'm going to need a 'yes, Josh'."

"Are you just testing that I know how to say, 'oh yes, Josh'?" I ask, putting needy breaths into my voice.

He clearly likes that. He lifts his hand and drags his thumb over my bottom lip. "I want to know you're completely with me here, and that you want everything I'm going to give you. But yeah. I want to hear a lot more of my name from these lips."

I nod but also say, "Yes, Josh. I will stop you at any point that I'm not comfortable."

He nods and puts his hands on the dip of my waist, running them up and down from the waistband of my jeans to the cups of my bra.

"And by the way," I say. "The same goes for you. You can stop anything you don't want to do."

He doesn't laugh that off. He nods. "I will."

Consent is so fucking sexy. And being with a man who wants it fully and understands that it goes both ways is amazing.

"So, here's what I'm thinking," he says conversationally as he continues to stroke up and down my sides, sending goosebumps skittering in every direction and making my nipples pebble hard behind my bra cups. "I strip you down to nothing, then I go to my knees, and I make you come at least once right out here in the hallway."

This blatant sex talk is so new to me. It's been a while since I've been with anyone, but I don't think I've ever been with anyone who talks about it so straightforwardly.

"You don't want to go to the bedroom?" I ask.

"Oh, Danger, I very much want to go to the bedroom," he says. "And I fully intend to take you in there. But I'm going to start out here. Because you've indicated that this pussy has been sadly neglected lately. Isn't that right?"

Oh…*God*.

Yes, it has, but his *words* are just making me feel things I haven't felt in a long time.

His hands pause on my waist. "Right?" he presses. "No one's worshipped you correctly in a long time?"

I drag in a shaky breath. "No."

"So you're going to let me eat your sweet pussy right here against the wall in the hallway where you'll think about it every time you walk past this spot. Right?"

Holy…

I swallow hard.

"Need to hear another, 'yes, Josh', here."

"Yes, Josh," I manage somehow without any air in my lungs.

He unbuttons and unzips my jeans and starts tugging them over my hips, dropping to his knees in front of me as he does it.

For some reason, despite what he said, this is the first time it really sinks in what he means.

"Wait," I say.

He looks up, his fingers tucked in the top of my jeans, jeans at my knees, him at eye level with the front of my panties. They do not match my bra. I buy pretty bras from time to time, but I don't usually buy bras and panty sets. Most of my panties are pretty basic. They're high cut on the legs, but they do go up over my stomach. I get them in a variety of colors—these are peach—but all are basic cotton.

I'm not sure I'm ready for Josh. Or maybe even any younger man. I'm sure he has seen better bodies than mine. Younger bodies, bodies that haven't had children yet. I'm not self-conscious about my body, and I'm not embarrassed to be naked with him. I'm just not sure that this is going to be what he thinks it's going to be. He told me himself he's never dated a single mom before.

"The hot, strong fireman can definitely put me up against the wall, right?" I ask, thinking I can have him skip this whole oral sex thing and we can just go straight to the good stuff. I don't need a lot of extra attention. And I probably don't need a lot of foreplay. It's been a while. I'm very ready.

He studies me from on his knees. "I could definitely do that. If that's what you want, that is what we'll do," he says.

I feel a little wave of relief. Followed by just a twinge of disappointment.

I have never been with a guy who loved going down on women, and I've definitely never been with one who was good at it. I have no idea if Josh would be good at it, but for some reason, I think I wouldn't mind finding out.

But I brush that off. Sex. That's all I need here. I am pretty sure he's going to be good at *that*. He's gorgeous, turns me on with just a smile, has a great body, and again, that five years between us could definitely make a difference here. The last guy I dated that I got naked with was actually seven years older than me. Which was great. He also had some relationship baggage and was used to real women's bodies. None of that fazed him.

But he was just good in bed. Not great. Not amazing. And beyond that there wasn't much reason for us to stay in a relationship.

"I would like that," I tell him. Being put up against the wall by those muscles? Yeah. That's something I would replay in my mind with my vibrator in the future.

"Okay. After." He continues tugging on my jeans.

"What?" I ask, instinctively lifting a foot so that he can slide one pant leg off my leg.

"After I give this pussy some special attention," he says.

Again, his dirty bluntness hits me in the gut with an explosion of heat that quickly spreads out and *down*.

"Oh," is all I can manage.

He looks up at me as he slides my other pant leg off, tossing my jeans away.

"How long has it been?" he asks.

"For sex? A long time."

It's been a long time for sex, but even longer for a man's mouth to be even where Josh's is right now.

"How about since you had an orgasm that wasn't battery powered?"

I grin in spite of my nerves. "Really long. You're in nearly virgin territory here."

He lifts a brow.

"Not really," I say. "Obviously."

"You've had orgasms, though? From men?" He almost seems *concerned.*

"Yes. But not every time, so it's been longer for that than for sex."

He mutters something that I don't quite make out. "But it's been a long time for you too, right?" I ask.

I can't forget that Ami told me about how he didn't even really flirt with women as far as she knew.

"Yes," he says with a huffed chuckle. "So *please* tell me that you're going to let me do this."

Is he actually begging me, literally on his knees, to *let* him go down on me?

I think quickly. "Maybe I should take a quick shower," I blurt out.

His eyebrows lift, but he slides his hands up my outer thighs, and I am so glad that I shaved this morning.

"If that's what you want to do, I'll wait." His hands slide back to cup my ass and hold me as he leans in and presses his nose against the front of my panties, inhaling deeply. "I want you to be comfortable. I want you to be able to fully relax and enjoy. But you do not need to shower for my sake."

My entire body feels like it's melting against the wall. Having his hands on me, his dirty words, honestly just being with him like this, and having him want this is enough to send electrified sparks up and down my body over every nerve ending.

"Just..."

He presses a kiss to the front of my panties, then looks up at me. "I get it. It's been a long time. It's hard to be intimate with people after you've been disappointed, or hurt, or even just gotten comfortable without it."

I nod. How can this young, hot guy, who could probably go out with just about any woman he meets, understand that?

"Are you sure you want this?" I ask.

"If we sleep together, if I fuck you well and make you mine this way, will you get clingy? Catch feelings? Want to see if this can turn into a real relationship?" he asks.

I decide to be honest. "Yes, very likely."

A pleased look crosses his face. "Then yes, I'm very sure I want to do this."

Dirty and romantic? I mean, sign me up.

"Okay," I tell him, taking a deep breath. "Just don't be surprised when this takes about ten seconds."

He chuckles and lifts his hands, hooking his thumbs in the top of my panties.

"I don't care how long it takes or what happens, I just want you to let go. Enjoy this. Let me figure out exactly how to make you crazy. I want every piece of you. But I will take them as slowly or as quickly as you wanna give them to me."

"Be careful how you talk to me," I tell him. "You might find yourself tied to my bed and me not letting you go in the morning."

He slides my panties down my legs, and I lift my feet so that he can get rid of them.

"Don't make promises you can't keep," he says.

He's now running his hands up and down the back of my legs, staring at my pussy.

"Who says I don't intend to keep it?" I ask breathlessly.

"Muriel," he says. "She'll hunt you down if I don't show up at the next challenge."

I laugh and thread my fingers through his hair. "You've got a point. She's terrifying."

"But I promise that whatever happens here that would prompt you to tie me up and keep me forever, I will happily do you over and over again. No bondage required." He pauses, then grins. "I mean no non-consensual bondage."

I laugh even as my breath feels trapped in my lungs. I pull my fingers through his hair. "We can save the restraints for another time."

He leans in and kisses my stomach. "I like you so fucking much, Danger."

"Same," I tell him softly.

He looks up at me, his lips still against my stomach. "Can I have you right here, now? Can I remind you what it feels like to have your pussy worshiped?"

I give a choked laugh. "I'm not sure that's ever happened, so nothing to remind me of."

Something flares in his eyes. "Then we are most definitely going to do that."

He kisses my stomach again, then kisses across to one of my hip bones. He gives me a little nip.

My lower stomach and pussy are already clenching. I force myself to breathe, or I'm going to pass out.

"Take your bra off for me," he says against my hipbone before he starts kissing a path down the crease of my hip to my inner thigh.

I reach up and fumble around with the hooks of my bra, my fingers suddenly clumsy. I finally get it undone and toss it to the floor. His face is hovering right in front of my clit, but he looks up, taking me in.

"Fucking gorgeous," he says roughly.

His hand slides back to cup my ass. "Do you like having your nipples played with?"

I swallow hard and can only nod.

"Then do it. Make yourself feel good."

I cup my breasts, kneading gently at first, but then, confidence, and yes, a surge of lust, hits me. I run my thumbs over my stiff nipples, feeling hot desire twist through me. He's watching me intently, and his gaze empowers me. I take one nipple between my thumb and forefinger, rolling it the way I like, sending arrows of heat straight to my clit.

"That's it," he praises in a gruff voice. "That's my girl."

Oh hell, that helps too. His girl? We've known each other for a day. But being here with him like this feels so natural. I pluck at my nipple again and squeeze the other side.

My pussy responds as usual.

"Keep going," he says. Then he leans in and, with just the tip of his tongue, teases over my clit.

"Oh God," I moan.

"Lots more of that," he says.

His next lick is firmer and longer, and my head thunks back against the wall.

He takes that as a sign of encouragement, which he should.

One hand slides to the back of my thigh, and he lifts my leg, hooking it over his shoulder and spreading me open.

Holy crap. I am spread wide, fully exposed, and now all I can think is *get your mouth on me now.*

It's like he can read my thoughts. He leans in, giving me a long, firm lick from slit to clit. He teases my clit with his tongue for a few seconds, circling and pressing, then he sucks. Gently at first, then with more pressure.

I almost forgot what I'm doing with my breasts. I squeeze my nipple, and my pussy clenches. All of this already has an orgasm coiling.

I am used to this not taking long. I turn my vibrator to setting three and don't have to worry about it being a long, drawn-out thing.

I don't know if my body is just primed that way now or if this man is just really that skilled with his tongue.

Either way, I'm really happy right now. I've lost all self-consciousness and any thoughts that good times need to be battery-powered. Josh knows what he's doing, and yeah, this is better than plastic. His mouth is hot and wet, and in addition, he is making noises that make little bursts of fire spark throughout my veins.

"Yes," he says against me. "You are fucking amazing. You're so delicious. I could stay here all night."

I love all of that, but he cannot stay there all night. Not like this. I need more.

So I decide to tell him that. He's not the only one who can be straightforward and blunt about these things.

"That's very nice," I tell him, practically panting. "But I'm not gonna let you do that. I'm going to need you to fuck me at some point."

He pauses as if I've surprised him, then he growls, the sound sending waves of lust through me. He sucks my clit into his mouth, hard, then slides two thick fingers into my pussy. He doesn't work up to it. He doesn't gently press with one finger first. He pumps his fingers deep and then spreads them wide.

"Oh my God, Josh!" I gasp.

"I fucking love hearing my name like that," he praises.

He sucks again and then curls his finger forward, finding that elusive spot that only one of my vibrators can hit.

And, okay, it took me more than ten seconds, but not much. My orgasm hits suddenly, not taking me up and over the rise steadily like happens with my vibrator, but all at once like a bomb detonating.

I grip his hair and squeeze my thighs together. Or I try to. But he's there, not letting me go, not letting up on the pressure.

He continues sucking and stroking, keeps the orgasm going for several long, delicious moments.

Finally, I slump back against the wall, and he eases his fingers out, sliding them into his mouth, and looks up at me.

I look down at him, kneeling before me, having just made me feel better than I have felt in probably years.

"Thank you," I say. Stupidly.

He grins around his fingers as he slides them free. "See? You are definitely dangerous."

I have a hand on my rapidly rising and falling chest. "Me?" I ask. "Right now, I would sign over my house to you, give you all the money in my bank account, and probably promise to bankroll a tropical vacation for you."

He grins and slides my leg off his shoulder, setting my foot on the floor. Then he slowly rises until our mouths are only a centimeter apart. "You are dangerous to everything I've known. I am addicted to you. And I can't see myself going back to a life where I'm not seeing you on a regular basis."

He's intense. This is going fast. He jumps all in all at once. He's warned me about this.

But I can't help it, I really fucking like that.

"Okay, fine, I'll bankroll two tropical vacations."

He chuckles. "All I need is for you to take me into your bedroom and for you to lie back on your bed and spread these pretty legs wide for me."

CHAPTER 14
JOSH

SHE'S A GODDESS.

She also has no idea what she's doing to me.

This is not a function of it having been so long since I was with a woman. It would be easy to chalk it up to that, but I've been with enough women in the past to know that this is different. She's different.

Thea Chabert is going to let me have her body and her heart. I can feel it. And I am not taking that lightly.

I'm also going to be fucking worthy of both.

Starting by giving this woman the best sex she has ever had.

She takes a deep breath, then takes my hand, threading our fingers together, and leads me down the hall, buck ass naked.

I want to keep her that way for the next week or so. That's not going to happen, of course. At least not right now. But as far as I'm concerned, we have weeks and months and years ahead of us. At some point, I might just have to make that tropical vacation come true somewhere she can not wear clothes for several days at a time.

She tugs me into her bedroom and straight to the bed. She lies back and spreads her legs just the way I asked.

"Good girl."

I see the way her eyes widen, but I trust that she'll tell me if she doesn't like that kind of shit.

Turns out she likes it a lot.

She cups her breasts, rolling both nipples, then slides her hand down over her stomach between her legs. She circles her clit.

"You have too many clothes on," she tells me.

I do, but I am struck dumb, watching her play with herself.

"Fuck, Danger, keep going."

She circles a little faster and wets her lips, but says, "I do this all the time. Now I have a hot, dirty-talking firefighter in my room? No way. Take your clothes off, Josh."

She has a point. "Rain check on watching you get yourself off, though," I tell her.

I'm aware I'm blunt when I talk about sex and fucking and pussies and other favorite topics. I think it took Thea a minute to catch up. But she's right with me now.

She slides a finger into her heat and says, "Okay. But that goes both ways."

I yank my shirt off and toss it somewhere to the side.

I rip open the button and zipper on my jeans. "You want to masturbate together? Finger your pussy while I jerk off? Come all over your pretty tits? Fuck yes. Sign me up."

Her cheeks are pink and she's breathing faster.

"Yes. I want everything."

"You can have everything and then a bunch of stuff you don't even know about."

She lifts a single brow, her finger stalling. "Do you think there are things I don't know about?"

I step out of my jeans and shuck off my boxer briefs.

I watch as she takes in everything about my naked body for the first time. I give her a second of unobstructed view, then wrap my hand on my cock. "Let's just say I look forward to finding out everything you know. I'll also happily teach you everything I know."

She laughs. "I love your cockiness. But you have no idea the stuff I read."

I put a knee on the bed between her legs. She instinctively widens them further. "I wanna hear more about this."

"I'll happily share my favorite spicy romances with you anytime."

I like the sound of that. "I have long shifts at the firehouse where there's sometimes not much to do. I could add to my to-be-read pile."

She grins up at me, almost more pleased by that answer than by the fact that I'm stroking a huge cock right in front of her.

"You'd read books with me? Dirty, filthy romances?"

I nod. "Hell yeah. I'd do a lot of things with you. Anything, actually."

She reaches for me. "You're too good to be true. But I'm going to enjoy every second until you show me that you do have a flaw."

I fall forward, catching myself with one outstretched hand, my other hand still wrapped around my cock. I need some pressure and friction there, or I'm going to explode.

"My major flaws are that I fall hard and fast, I often leap before I look, and I love a thrill. I also sometimes—often—use things up in the kitchen and forget to put them on the list to buy more. Oh, and I suck at remembering to call if I'm stuck at work longer than expected."

She runs her hands over my shoulders, up my neck, to the back of my head. She smiles. "I can actually deal with all of those things. I mean, I come with a twelve-year-old, a very involved family, and an over-the-top hometown."

"I love all of them," I tell her sincerely. "I'm not saying they won't be a bit of a pain sometimes, but hey, I haven't told you about my family yet."

She laughs. "I actually can't wait to find out."

I am falling in love with this woman. I mean, I knew that

yesterday. I think she's maybe catching on as well. But it's official. And after I fuck her, I'm not going to be getting over her.

"IUD, right?" I ask, rubbing the head of my cock over her clit.

She sucks in a little breath and nods.

"I haven't been with anybody in a long time. During the last check-up, everything was negative," I tell her.

She nods. "Same."

I have a hard time taking a deep breath, but I have to ask, "Can I fuck you bare?"

"Oh God, yes."

"You're sure? I think I have condoms in my toiletry bag."

She shakes her head, her hair spilling out against the duvet. "No. Like this. You and me."

I lean in and capture her mouth, kissing her deeply. This is fucking. I am going to make us both feel very good. There will be hard orgasms. But this is more. I have real feelings for this woman, and this is the first of many times that we're going to connect. Physically and otherwise.

"Then wrap your legs around me and let me into the sweet pussy."

She complies, lifting her legs, crossing her ankles at my lower back as I guide my cock into her heat.

Fuck. This won't last long. It's been too long, and I want her too much. But she's right there with me.

As I try to go slow, her legs tighten around me, her heels digging into my ass. She lifts her hips and gasps my name.

"Easy, I've got you. Give me a second," I say, gritting my teeth.

I want to pound into her. I want to take her. Claim her.

"More," she begs. "Please. Harder."

"Fuck, *Thea*."

"Josh! Please!"

"You want it harder? You need me deep, Danger?"

"Yes! God, yes!"

I let go. I pump into her deep and fast. She cries out, but her body grips me, fingers digging into my sides, her legs tight around my hips, her pussy squeezing me, keeping me close as I fuck her hard.

"Yes, Josh! Oh, God, like that!"

I tip my hips, press into her, rubbing her clit as I stroke deep, and I feel her clench hard.

"Oh, yes! Yes!" she chants.

"You're perfect," I praise. "So perfect. I'm going to get lost in you over and over."

"This is so good."

"It's just the start. This pussy is mine now."

Surprisingly, that tips her over the edge. She cries out my name as her pussy milks me.

I grip one hip, my other arm shaking as I hold myself above her and thrust faster. Then I come so hard that my freaking toes curl. I'm not kidding.

I hold myself there, buried deep, breathing hard.

I stare down at Thea.

She is breathing hard, but she has a happy, contented look on her face.

"Fuck, girl. That was...I'm ruined."

She covers her face and laughs.

I pull her hand away. "What?"

"I was just going to say something but...I shouldn't."

I grin even though I don't know what she's thinking about. "Say it."

"No."

I lean in, putting my mouth against her ear. "I have ways of making you talk."

She shivers. "Well, *that's* not going to make me spill it easily." She shifts her hips against me.

I'm getting hard again. I press into her. "Say it."

She feels me too, and her brows rise. "Oh, to be young..."

I laugh. "Don't worry, you can just lie there and take it." I pull back and thrust gently, letting her feel that I'm ready to go again.

Her breath catches, and she widens her legs.

"That's my girl. Take whatever I've got to give you, *whenever* I want to give it to you," I say gruffly.

She moans and lifts her hips.

"Do you feel what you do to me?" I ask, pressing my forehead against hers. "I haven't even turned you over, or made you straddle me, or seen how much of my cock you take past these pretty lips."

"Oh, God." She wraps her arms around my neck and lifts to meet my next thrust. "I was going to say I'm glad you're ruined, because this is *my* cock now."

And *that* is why I'm still fucking her when our phones beep with texts.

Downstairs.

So we don't see the messages until we have only ten minutes to clean up, get dressed, and get to Perks and Rec for Christmas Carol Karaoke, the second surprise challenge of the day.

CHAPTER 15
THEA

HAVING a twelve-year-old who has friends I have no qualms about her staying overnight with is amazing.

Most times, it means I get to lie around on the couch alone, eat raw cookie dough straight from the tube for dinner, and binge-watch *The Righteous Gemstones* with no alarm clock set for the next morning.

This time, it means waking up next to a naked fireman.

I really like raw cookie dough and Adam DeVine, but this beats all of those Saturday nights.

"Do you want the leftover pecan rolls?" I ask as I tip my head to the right so Josh has better access to the spot on my neck that he's kissing.

The hand he has under the hem of my T-shirt, stroking back and forth across my bare stomach, inches higher. I put clothes on—well, a T-shirt and panties—to come down to the kitchen, but he didn't wait for me to come back to bed. He came after me.

"I am definitely hungry for something soft and sweet, but you said you had something else for me, I believe. Want me to make some requests, or did you have something specific in mind?"

"I did have something in mind, but I love your dirty mouth, so why don't you tell me what you're thinking?" I ask.

"Sure," he says conversationally as he cups one breast, pluck-ing, then tugging on my nipple in a way that sends ripples of heat to my pussy. "I want to lift you up on this breakfast bar, strip this T-shirt and these panties off of you and feast on your warm, sweet cunt—"

My gasp and giggle cut him off.

He chuckles against my neck. "How has no one talked dirty to you like this before?"

"I don't know. You're scandalizing me."

"I cannot keep from thinking about and talking about this body and everything I want to do to it," he says, sliding his hand from my breast, over my stomach, and between my thighs, where he cups me, bringing me back against his hard body.

He's in jeans, but they are unbuttoned and unzipped, resting loosely on his hips, and he's shirtless. I want to run my hands and tongue all over every ridge and plane of his shoulders, chest, back, and abs. I want to trace every line of his tattoos and hear what each means.

I could easily reach back and slip my hand inside the front of his jeans and underwear. I know I would find him thick and hard. I've never especially loved giving oral sex, but I have the sudden urge to sink to my knees for this man.

I turn on the stool and look up at him. "All day today, while we are supposed to be doing fun and sweet Christmas activities with two eccentric but adorable little old ladies, every time you smile, I'm going to think about how much I want your lips on my clit."

His eyes are hot, but he grins as he cups the back of my neck in one big hand, the rough pad of his thumb, stroking up and down the side of my throat. "Are you trying to scandalize *me*, Danger?"

I nod. "How was that?"

"Amazing. Keep it up."

"Every time I look at it, I'm going to think about how your ass feels under my hands when I'm gripping it while you're thrusting into me."

He looks pleased and very turned on. His thumb pauses under my jaw, pressing slightly to tip my head back. He leans in, his mouth hovering over mine. "Is that because I am going to be in front of you all day? Winning?"

I laugh, but then have no choice but to pull him in and kiss him.

Just as the kiss turns hungry, my phone pings with a text.

I sigh and pull back. We're still in the middle of Merry Mayhem. That text could be anything. It could be my daughter, too. As much as I would love to be Josh's breakfast buffet, I need to be responsible.

I note that his phone does not vibrate, so this isn't a surprise challenge text.

It's from Nora, though.

Nora: *No morning surprise challenge. You're welcome.*

Nora: *I assume you were up late. *winky emoji* You didn't want to get up early.*

Nora: *By the way, I totally noticed how you and Josh were looking at each other last night. I don't think I was the only one. You guys need to watch it. It was VERY obvious.*

I smile, but then that fully sinks in, and my stomach flips over. I look up at Josh.

"No morning challenge. Nora's gift to us. She assumed we were up late."

Josh grins. "I really like Nora."

I nod. "But she says we were a little obvious last night."

He shrugs. "Probably. It's going to get harder and harder to hide how we feel. But she already knows about us. It's just more obvious to her."

"That's probably part of it," I agree. "But we need to be careful."

"You're right," he says with a sigh. "But this can't go on much longer."

I completely agree and want to come up with a solution, but

I'm distracted by his naked torso, the fact that we have a little extra time now this morning, and…

A new text comes in on my phone.

This is from my mom.

She's awake!!!

My breath catches in my throat. My eyes immediately well with tears.

"What's wrong?" Josh asks, noticing instantly.

I look up at him. "Violet's awake."

He doesn't look shocked. "That's awesome. That's about the right timing."

Another text comes in from my mom.

Everything looks fantastic! All vitals and tests are normal. No memory loss!

I repeat the message to Josh.

His smile is genuine. "That's wonderful news. She'll probably be coming home in the next couple of days. She'll have some precautions for a short time, but it sounds like she's going to be back to normal quickly."

I'm so relieved. I believed him all along when he said that she was going to be okay. But having her awake and everything coming out normal, I feel a huge weight lifted off my chest. I don't think I realized how worried I was.

I am, of course, familiar with concussion protocols. I know that for the next few days, Violet will need to limit her screen time, excessive activity, and anything that requires a lot of cognitive effort. But if things continue to improve and she feels good, she will slowly return to her normal activities and routine. She is young, healthy, and seems to be coming through this well. She shouldn't have any permanent effects.

"We should go and see her," I say. I already feel bad that I haven't been there. My whole family, and all of my friends, have encouraged me to stay in Rebel and have assured me it's fine. And I know, practically, that it is. It still feels weird.

"Yes, for sure," Josh agrees. "We also need to let her know what's going on with us."

I consider that. We do. She definitely needs to know before anyone else figures it out.

I don't want to keep this from my family or any more of my friends. But it's only fair to fill Violet in first.

"I'm going to head up and take a shower and get dressed," I say, sliding off the stool.

"I could join you," Josh says, not giving me much space.

I smile up at him. "If you join me, we're never going to make it out of this house."

I can tell he likes that. "We actually don't have time to get to New Orleans, see her, and get back," he says, glancing at the clock.

Dammit, he's right. Even without a surprise challenge, we have to be downtown for the obstacle course at ten. "Okay, I'm going to tell Nora about Violet. She won't schedule a surprise challenge between the obstacle course and the gingerbread building challenge this afternoon. We can go see her in between those."

"Great plan," he says. "Maybe we'll even get a chance to see her just the two of us."

Yeah, I'm going to have to find a way to distract any other visitors so that Josh can talk to Violet about what's going on under the guise of being a concerned boyfriend who wants a few minutes alone with her.

Crap, this is so complicated. Even to tell Violet the truth, we're going to have to fib to the rest of the family for a short time.

We want to tell everyone the full story, but Violet needs to be a part of that.

We clean up and dress separately, then head for the high school, where the obstacle course is set up.

A lot of people have already arrived, and the general atmosphere is festive.

Muriel and Patty are already there, of course.

Patty is wearing a lavender tracksuit, bright white tennis shoes, and has a lavender scarf around her hair that matches her lavender sunglasses.

Muriel has a turquoise tracksuit that's so bright it could easily be seen from six blocks away. Her tennis shoes are hot pink, the baseball cap on her head is sunshine yellow, and she has bright blue goggles covering her eyes. They look like swim goggles, but I suppose they probably make goggles for biking or other outdoor activities. In any case, they are blue plastic with clear plastic centers and a wide blue strap that secures them on her head. The strap makes her hair stick up in all directions, reminding me of white dandelion puff.

"Good morning!" Patty greets with a huge smile.

"Good morning, ladies," I say. "Are you ready for this?"

I look around, trying to find Andi. I trust my friend to come up with something to help the ladies get around, and since I haven't heard from her, I assume the plan is on track.

"This is going to be great," Muriel says, surprisingly perky.

"You stretched and hydrated?" Josh asks her, holding out his fist.

She bumps his fist and then says, "I've had four cups of coffee and I don't need to stretch. My chariot awaits, and I have a big, strong charioteer here."

Josh glances at me with a confused frown, and I shrug.

"Chariot?" I ask. "Does this mean you've seen Andi this morning?"

"Yup. She's right over there." Muriel points slightly past my shoulder, and Josh and I both turn.

Andi and Everly are headed in our direction.

And they're each pushing a shopping cart.

Or what used to be shopping carts.

My eyes get wider even as my grin grows.

My friend is a genius.

"What do you think?" Andi asks. "I got inspired and just

forged ahead. But I knew you were busy at karaoke last night, so Everly came over to help and give me some input."

I circle around the two carts and my friends. "I am amazed."

"You just cut off the fronts?" Josh asks.

Andi nods. "Cut off the back of the baskets to where they widen a bit and removed the little seat where they put kids," she says. "Then glammed up the whole thing."

She's not kidding.

The shopping carts are basically intact except for being open on the front. But they've been painted. One is shiny gold. The other is bright pink with, I swear, glitter mixed in.

Both baskets are now padded with cushions along the bottom and all sides. The gold one has black cushions, the pink has purple cushions. There are also embellishments. Draped along the outside of the gold cart are black, gold, and purple beads. The pink cart has multicolored scarves threaded in and out of the basket.

"You can get in and out of this easily?" I ask Patty.

Patty steps forward and slips into the gold cart as if she's sitting down on a chair. "No problem," she says.

Muriel also demonstrates how easy it is for her to sit into her cart and then get back out.

"And check this out," Patty says, bending over and pushing a button on the wooden box that has been secured to the platform underneath the basket on her cart.

Christmas music starts playing.

"You even gave her a stereo?" Josh asks with a laugh.

"Of course," Andi says with a grin. "I'm thinking these could be used again in the future."

"Check out what mine has," Muriel says, bending and opening the little door on the front of the wooden box under her cart. She reaches inside and pulls out a bag of gummy candy. "Snack box."

I notice one other addition. I step forward and pull on the piece of nylon that's tucked behind the back cushion. A bar extends, and the nylon slides over the top of the basket, providing a canopy.

"These are convertible chariots," I say with a laugh. "Brilliant."

"Wouldn't want the queens getting sunburned or sprinkled on," Andi says with a wink at Patty and Muriel.

"We are still trying to get Andi to tell us how much this costs," Patty says. "We are absolutely paying her for this."

Andi shakes her head. "Most of the stuff was just pieces and parts I had lying around in the studio. It was fun to put them together."

Patty puts a hand up, stopping Andi. "Absolutely not. I'm going to have Muriel keep working on you. I know she'll wear you down."

I know that Muriel will get Andi to the point where Andi will give her a number. The number won't be accurate, though. It will be way less than these two carts are worth, but there will come a point where Andi will want to shut Muriel up.

"Well, this is going to be amazing." I look at Josh. "Though I think you might be right about having the bigger, stronger charioteer," I tell Muriel.

"Prepare to eat our dust," Muriel says, settling into her shopping cart like a true royal.

We have about ten minutes until the obstacle course starts, so we push the carts over to the starting line, and Josh asks if I want some hot chocolate.

I'm contemplating if I can finish a whole cup of hot liquid before I have to run up and down this football field when I hear our names being called.

"Thea! Josh!"

We both turn at the sound of my mother's voice.

What the…

Shock washes over me.

My mom, dad, both grandfathers, and my daughter are all striding toward us with huge grins.

But I don't focus on any of them.

I only have eyes for my sister.

"Violet!" Andi exclaims.

Andi and Everly both look at me. "Violet's here? Why didn't you tell us?" Everly asks.

I don't even realize that I have reached out and grabbed Josh's hand until he squeezes mine. "Breathe. It's gonna be okay," he says softly.

I pull my eyes away from my gorgeous, upright, *conscious* sister and look up at him.

Of course, it's going to be alright. Violet is here. She is obviously out of the hospital and doing well.

My family is surrounding her, and my dad has her arm tucked in his, but she's walking on her own. She is wearing sunglasses, but otherwise doesn't even show signs that she's been in the hospital with a serious concussion. In a fucking coma.

I realize quickly that my family was trying to surprise me with this.

Clearly, they woke Violet up yesterday. There's no way they brought her out of the coma and then let her come home within the past hour or two.

As they get closer, Violet looks from me to Josh, and her smile gets even bigger.

And that's when I realize they weren't trying to surprise *me*.

They were trying to surprise Violet's *boyfriend*.

"Hi!" she exclaims.

I step forward, instantly putting my arms around her. "Oh my God, Violet, I am so thrilled to see you."

She hugs me tightly. "Me too."

"Are you really okay? How do you feel?"

"I actually feel really good." She pulls back and looks at me. "I woke up yesterday. I know Mom and Dad didn't tell you. That's on me. I wanted to..." She glances at Josh. "I wanted to see you here, not at the hospital."

She's talking to him. She didn't want *him* to see her in the hospital.

"I know that's silly," she says, laughing lightly. She pulls back from me to face him. "I mean, you're the one who pulled me out of the car. You saw me at the worst of it."

I realize I'm not breathing, and I force myself to take a deep inhale of oxygen.

"You look fantastic," Josh says, his deep voice, low and reassuring.

She does. Violet is beautiful, even only one day post-coma.

She tucks her hair behind her ear. "Thanks." She's acting almost shy.

Out of the corner of my eye, I see a crowd gathering around us. The entire town. Of course.

Violet has lived here her whole life. Everyone knows her. This entire town has been worried about her, and I'm sure they are thrilled to see her.

The crowd also includes her ex. Sam and Ashley are about ten feet away and can likely hear everything. They can certainly see everything now that Josh and Violet are center stage.

Which is good.

Probably.

This entire thing, with Josh being here for Merry Mayhem in the first place, is because Sam is here with Ashley.

It's dramatic, and happy, and worthy of a TV Christmas movie.

I nudge Josh with my elbow.

Thankfully, he's a very smart man, and he instantly understands.

He steps forward with a big grin and enfolds Violet in a hug.

She seems to sag in relief, wrapping her arms around his waist and squeezing tight.

"I'm so glad you're here," she says to him.

"I'm glad you're here too," he tells her.

"Thank you so much for doing Merry Mayhem anyway," she says.

They're speaking softly enough now that I am probably the only one who can hear them.

"Of course. I made you a promise," Josh says.

Violet pulls back and looks up at him with a sweet smile. "I've been thinking, my family has told me all about how great you've been with everything, and how much they love you, and how fun all of this is. And I think…" She wet her lips, then says in a rush, "We should do this for real."

I stiffen, my gaze flying to Josh's face.

He is clearly surprised, but he quickly covers it. "Do what?"

"Date. For real."

Then my sister lifts up on tiptoe and presses her lips to Josh's.

CHAPTER 16
JOSH

WELL.

Shit.

That is not how a man should react when a beautiful woman is kissing him, of course. Especially when that woman is supposed to be his *girlfriend*.

But that's exactly what this situation calls for.

This is Violet, not Thea. I should not be kissing anyone but Thea. Ever.

Fuck.

What can I do, though?

This entire town, her entire family, thinks we're together. *She* thinks we're together, or, I guess, that we should be, and since I haven't had a chance to talk to her about it, so…

I go with it.

Even as I'm cringing inside.

I do not prolong the kiss, though. It's five seconds, maybe.

Despite the pressure of her hand on the back of my head, I disengage. "We need to talk about this," I say quietly.

I'm very aware that Sam and Ashley are standing only a few feet away.

Everyone is. I don't want to expose this as a lie to anyone without talking to Violet first, but definitely not in front of the ex.

"Sure, I can't wait," Violet says, her smile bright.

"Okay, Casanova, we need to go," Muriel says, tugging on my sleeve.

Thank goodness.

Violet lets me go. I immediately look for Thea, but she's turned away and is in discussion with Patty, I assume about their strategy for the upcoming race.

I follow Muriel to the starting line, and she sits down in her sparkly pink cart. "You better focus," she says, giving me a frown.

"What do you mean? I'm focused."

She shakes her head. "I don't have time for you to work through a love triangle while I'm trying to win this obstacle course."

"It's not a love triangle," I insist. I look side to side. We can *not* have people think that. "It's not…like that."

"Now you're just insulting me," Muriel says, adjusting her goggles and wiggling on her cushions. "I've seen how you look at Thea."

Dammit.

"How do I look at Thea?"

"Like she's everything you ever asked Santa for," Muriel says.

Well…fuck. That's exactly how she makes me feel.

"You're smiling like I'm brilliant," Muriel says.

"You're…insightful," I say.

She points a finger at me. "*Stop* looking at your girlfriend's sister like that."

"It's not like that," I say again.

"Then stop kissing your girlfriend," she says.

I sigh. "I've never kissed Violet. Well, before just now. It's complicated, Muriel."

Muriel narrows her eyes. "I like you, Josh."

"Thank you, I like you too."

"But that woman?" She points at Patty. "The one I drive nuts and fight with daily and know *everything* about, even things I wish I didn't know?"

"Yeah."

"Choosing a man over her would be the worst decision I ever made. I would *never* do that." She crosses her arms. "Not twice in one lifetime anyway."

Ah.

"Do *not* do that to Thea and Violet," she tells me. "Not if you even think you care about one, or both, of them."

I nod. "I don't want to. That's…" I sigh. "That's not what this is."

But if Violet wants to try dating, thinks this could be something based on…what? Me rescuing her? What her family has told her?…does that make this a love triangle?

Fuck.

"Fine," Muriel finally says. "Just promise me that you'll follow Thea's lead. Don't make her choose."

I swallow. Then nod. "Okay."

"Good boy."

"Okay, everyone!" Nora says from the stage. "As has been pointed out to me, our rules don't specifically state that in the obstacle course, partners have to alternate like they do in the relay race. Which means that both partners can participate in some of the obstacles, or one partner can do multiple obstacles in a row. Obviously, our rules are a little looser than I realized," Nora sighs, but she's smiling, and the crowd laughs. "But I don't care! This is about having fun, not strictly adhering to a bunch of stringent rules."

"That should be the new motto. All fun, no rules," someone calls.

That gets applause and more laughter.

Nora beams. "Great idea. I love that. Anyway, basically as long as both partners are here and participating to some extent, the obstacle course is whatever it's gonna be," she says, spreading one arm wide.

There's more applause in response to that.

I like this town. It's pretty laid-back. Yes, they seem to like their entertainment a little wacky, but they do seem to be in it for a good time more than anything else.

"And with that, ready, set, go!" Nora calls.

The jingle bells jingle, and we all run for the first obstacle.

Or, rather, I run while pushing Muriel, who is whooping like she's riding a bucking bronco.

It's only about a twenty-foot sprint, but we get there a few steps ahead of Thea and Patty, but a couple of steps behind Beckett and Sutton.

The first "obstacle" is more like one of the stations on the relay race.

There are six frosted sugar cookies and a glass of milk. The cookies look familiar, so I'm guessing they're the ones we all decorated the day before. Muriel grabs a cookie, I grab another, and we start chewing as fast as we can.

I eat four while Muriel gobbles two. We share the milk. Then it's onto the next obstacle.

Now this one is more like it.

This is Candy Cane Lane. It is a winding path made of white and red striped cardboard with six-foot-tall plastic candy canes dotted at various intervals down the middle. We have to zigzag through the candy canes, picking up mini wrapped candy canes as we go—I'm going to assume whoever has the most at the end gets additional points—and avoiding the little elves that dart out from behind fake trees, cardboard chimneys, and giant stockings along the sides.

The elves are kids, literally dressed in elf costumes, and they clearly think this is the most fun ever. They giggle and wait until someone is nearing where they're hiding before they jump out, obviously trying to be as in the way as possible.

Muriel begins making honking noises. I'm trying to shoo them out of the way, but the kids find that even more of a challenge, and we end up with two running in slow motion right in front of us.

By the time we're finished with the lane, Muriel says, "The next one you do by yourself. Park me to the side."

"Are you sure?"

She points, and I realize there's no way for me to take her through the Tinsel Tunnel in her cart. I'm going to have to crawl through on hands and knees.

"Okay, but how are you going to get to the next obstacle?"

"I've got her," Mitchell—at least I think it's Mitchell—says as he and Max run up to the tunnel.

Max has already hit his hands and knees and started through the tunnel, so I simply nod, figuring all's fair, and follow Max in.

I start on hands and knees, crawling through the curtains of tinsel and trying to avoid putting my hands in whatever the wet, chunky, sticky stuff is that's spaced throughout the tunnel. I'm tempted to smell or taste it, but I don't have time.

I also quickly realize that the tunnel gets shorter and shorter, and by the end, I am army crawling on my belly. And unable to completely avoid the wet, sticky stuff that, now that my nose is closer to it, smells like apple cinnamon and is possibly pie filling. Could be *a lot* worse.

When I emerge, I find that I'm not just behind Max but also Jesse, Beckett, and Thea. And tied with Sam.

Ashley stepped up and pushed Patty from the beginning of the tunnel to the end. She hands Sam a wet wipe and takes off toward the next obstacle.

Thea shoots me an indecipherable look as she grabs the back of Patty's cart and starts after Ashley.

Our goal is to beat Sam and Ashley, but I suddenly have an inkling that Thea very much wants to beat me and Muriel.

At least me.

The next obstacle again allows Muriel to participate. She instantly grabs a handful of the popcorn in the bowl on the table and starts eating.

But I pause with my hand to my mouth, realizing no one else is chewing.

"Muriel, I don't think we're supposed to eat it."

She stops and looks down the length of the table. "Oh, for fuck sake," she mutters. "I've always hated stringing popcorn."

But she picks up one end of the thread on the table in front of us and threads a needle onto it while I grab the other end and do the same. We both begin threading popcorn onto our string, alternating with cranberries, as quickly as possible.

But we are now behind Ashley and Sam, and Thea and Patty.

In fact, Thea and Patty have now pulled ahead of everyone. It's clear that Max and Mitchell have never threaded popcorn before, or even threaded needles before. Muriel grabs one and quickly attaches the thread. Patty threads Max's.

By the time our string is filled, we're behind Jesse and Brad, as well as Beckett and Sutton.

I sprint to the next obstacle and find that again, Muriel's going to have to sit this one out. I look at Max. "You've got her?"

He grins. "Sure."

Mitchell is already halfway up the climbing wall in front of us. Beckett's already at the top.

The objective here is to climb the wall, get the sack of presents away from the "Grinch" at the top, and climb back down the other side.

Piece of cake. In fact, I pass Brad on my way up. But Thea clears the top when I've still got a few feet to go.

"One massage and two pans of pecan rolls," she is saying to her "Grinch" when I crawl out on top.

"Three pans and two massages," he counters.

"No way."

There are ten "Grinches" up here, one for each pair, I assume. They're, of course, actually townspeople dressed in green furry coats.

Thea is negotiating with hers, but Beckett has a huge inflatable sword drawn and is literally battling his Grinch.

I look at the guy standing in front of me. "What am I supposed to do here?" The big red plastic bag of presents I'm supposed to retrieve is on the ground right in front of him.

"Well, you can try to fight me for it," he says with a grin. "Or you can negotiate."

He's shorter, thinner, and older than me. I'm not going to fight him. Even after he points to the giant inflatable mallets lying nearby.

"If you fight, you get bonus points."

Dammit. But I don't have time. Beckett is already running away with his sack of gifts. And his bonus points. "If we negotiate, what do you want?" I ask.

He shrugs. "What do you have?"

"Fifty bucks?"

He laughs. "Can't be money."

That's probably a good rule. "I…" I'm having trouble thinking of something. If his house was on fire, I'd be his guy. Or if he was bleeding profusely from…anywhere.

"You know how to paint a garage door?" he asks.

"Never done it, but guessing I could figure it out."

"That's what I want. An assist on the garage door next weekend."

"Done."

He bends, grabs the bag at his feet, and tosses it to me.

Okay, that was easy enough. I look down the line. Is everyone else getting favors and baked goods?

Nope. Mitchell has gigantic inflatable boxing gloves on his hands and is fighting his Grinch. I grin. I wish I could hang out and watch.

"What's your name?" I ask my Grinch.

"Dave. Don't worry, I'll come find you, Josh."

Chuckling, I sprint across the ten-foot expanse that they somehow built up and decorated to look like the top of a mountain, then climb down the other side.

Thea is right in front of me.

"Hey," I say to her. "We need to talk."

She gives me a look of disbelief. "You have to be kidding me."

"I'm not. Come on."

"Not now." She jumps off the bottom rung of the ladder-turned-mountain-side and sprints over to five gigantic wrapped gift boxes.

Each has holes in the top, and I watch as she digs in her bag, pulls out one of the gifts inside, then tosses it toward the hole in the top of the box that is wrapped similarly.

It bounces off the edge and, swearing, she goes to retrieve it, goes back to the yellow line that I just now notice on the ground, and tries again. This time the gift goes in the box.

"Do you want me to toss those gifts in the box?" Muriel calls to me.

"Do you want to?" I ask her.

She gives me a book that clearly says that's a stupid question. "Chuck those gifts in that box! Let's go!" she tells me.

She's right. I was so intent on studying Thea that I just now realize everyone else has thrown at least one gift, if not more, into the boxes.

I toss a box. It goes in on my first try.

"You seem upset," I say as Thea's second gift bounces off the edge of the box.

"Not now, Josh, seriously."

"Promise me we'll talk about this later."

"I'm not really sure what there is to talk about. Violet is back, you're supposed to be her boyfriend. The entire town believes that, so you have to play the part. End of discussion."

"But we're going to talk to her about it."

Thea suddenly turns to me, one hand on her hip. "You kissed her."

We're keeping our voices low so no one can hear what we're saying, especially over the general cheering and laughter as people try to toss their smaller gifts into the big gift boxes.

"I did not," I say. "She kissed me."

"You kissed her back."

"I *let her* kiss me," I admit. "But what was I supposed to do? I couldn't really react any other way right then."

Thea turns back toward the box and tosses her smaller gift. It goes in this time.

"That's my point," she says.

I turn to her. "What is?"

"Her being back and you kissing her in front of everyone, her being so excited to see you, her recovery and return here in the middle of Merry Mayhem, it's all just solidified this story that you're her boyfriend. My family loves you, and they've been building you up to her. The town loves you, and they're so excited that you're Violet's boyfriend."

"Won't they be just as excited that I'm *your* boyfriend?"

"When we break my sister's heart? Are you kidding?"

"But that's not going to happen. Violet and I aren't together. There's no heart to be broken."

"But now she wants to be with you!"

I take a step closer to Thea. "I will talk to her. I will tell her what happened and how I feel about you. Then we will tell *everyone* the truth."

"That's going to make her look so bad in front of Sam," Thea argues. "You're here to help her get through having her ex here with his new fiancée," she adds. "How is it going to help her when she has to admit that you were her *fake* boyfriend?"

Okay, that's fair. "What do you want to do?" I ask. "I can't change how I feel about you. I don't want to be with Violet."

"I don't know, Josh," she says. "I don't think there is a way to fix this."

My heart thuds hard in my chest. I step closer again. "Don't say that. That's ridiculous. Nothing is actually going on with Violet and me. We'll just wait till Sam leaves town—"

"That will build up Violet's hopes. She wants to try dating you for real."

"That's up to me too, Thea," I say, frowning. "We'll let her in on the truth. Even if we wait for Sam to leave town, we have to tell Violet the truth."

"But Sam will eventually find out."

"Find out what?" I am beyond frustrated. I want to grab her, hug her, kiss her, and remind her of the feelings between us.

"That Violet's boyfriend broke up with her for her sister! That's probably worse than her not having a boyfriend here at all."

I frown. "So…what do you want to do?"

"You go through with the plan. You continue to pretend to be Violet's boyfriend."

"And what about after Merry Mayhem?"

"Well, I don't know what you and Violet planned after that."

"We didn't plan anything after that. She had a car accident and ended up in a coma."

Thea looks like I slapped her, and I immediately regret my words." I'm sorry. I just mean—"

"My sister is awesome. I'm guessing that if you did Merry Mayhem together, you would have wanted to keep dating her afterward."

My heart bumps again, but this time it's with panic. "What are you saying?"

"I don't know. Maybe you and Violet do need to see—"

Now I cut *her* off. "No fucking way. I don't want Violet. I want you."

"I don't know how to work this out."

"So what? This is just over?"

"Yeah, I think so."

Suddenly, bells start ringing, and there is cheering all around us.

We both startle, obviously forgetting that there is an event going on—that we're supposed to be participating in—and that there are other people around us.

I hear the *boom* of the confetti canon, but it's in the distance.

We turn to see Muriel and Patty pushing their own carts toward the finish line.

Without us.

And well behind everyone else.

Thankfully, this gift toss is in the middle of the football field, so our conversation has taken place in private for the most part.

Since every other contestant passed us several minutes ago.

"Well fuck," Thea sighs.

And that pretty much sums it all up.

CHAPTER 17
THEA

EVERYONE WANTS to talk to Violet after the first challenge, and they all head to Perks and Rec for lunch. It seems the entire town packs into my grandfather's charming little coffee shop/ café/ bar.

Thank God.

It's so busy that I end up helping take orders and deliver food, which keeps me moving and too distracted to obsess over Josh sitting next to Violet with Harley, Leo, Brewser, and Wilson, smiling and acting the part of the doting boyfriend.

I could tell Josh wanted to get me alone when we first arrived at the café, and was frustrated to have no chance to talk to me, but what good would that do? There's nothing more to say. I don't know a way out of this without someone getting hurt. If it's me or someone I love, then I'll pick me every time.

He's here to help Violet. Nothing he and I do or say about a relationship between us helps Violet.

Sam is still here with his new fiancée. Literally up in front of everyone, her diamond sparkling in the sunshine and twinkle lights. I was actually glad Josh was beside Violet when Sam approached her—after the kiss, of course—to tell her he was so glad she was okay. Even if it killed me a little to watch Josh slip an arm around her waist when she put hers around him.

Every move like that just goes further to confirm them as a couple to the town.

"You okay?" Nora asks me after I deliver the last burger and BLT.

We're now leaning against the wall near the door to the kitchen in case Bruce needs to yell for help.

I shake my head. "Nope."

"You fell for him that fast?" my cousin asks.

What's the point of denying it? "Yep."

"You're really going to be okay with him dating V?"

I laugh. "Absolutely not. I'm hoping they break up, and I never have to see him again."

That's not nice of me, but I'm not sure how I'll survive seeing him with Violet across my parents' dinner table for the rest of my life.

Actually, I'm sure I *won't* survive.

If they don't move away, I'll have to.

Nora's quiet for a moment. "You know, I love the new Merry Mayhem motto. I might expand it to everything Parks and Recreation does."

"Motto?" I ask, looking over at her. What are we talking about?

"The all fun, no rules thing," she says.

Ah. I laugh. She's so transparent. "We need rules, Nora. They keep us safe."

Rules like not breaking your sister's heart if you can help it and sisters before misters, for instance.

"Well, sure, sometimes. But if rules keep us safe but unhappy, are they really good?" Nora asks. "They need to at least be revised, right? Like letting Patty and Muriel compete in the obstacle course with partners who would push them in amazing chariots when they couldn't run or walk the course."

"Chariots?" I ask, instead of commenting on the rest, because my chest feels really tight.

"Better word than cart," she says with a grin. "Plus, those things are *chariots*."

I smile, but then sigh. "What's your point?"

"On the surface, not stealing a man from your sister is a very good rule."

"I didn't—"

She holds up a hand to stop me. "But it also seems obvious that people should be able to do an obstacle course in order to, you know, participate in an obstacle course. But sometimes, you look closer and dig deeper, and it's not that straightforward, and *communicating* about the rules and how a rule is actually not good in a certain situation for everyone is a really good idea."

"How can this be *good* for Violet?" I ask.

"Not sure. But you could ask *her*. Maybe see if she's got a grocery cart you can paint pink."

"I—"

"It's a metaphor," she says.

I laugh. "Not a great one."

"I think it made my point."

I look across the café to where Josh and Violet are sitting.

They're getting up. Together. Just them.

And my first thought isn't that they're leaving together because he's chosen her. Instead, it's *he's going to see if she has a grocery cart we can use to get through this.*

"Maybe your metaphor isn't terrible," I tell Nora.

She gives me a bright smile. "Thank you."

CHAPTER 18
JOSH

IT'S VERY easy to get Violet alone since everyone assumes that I'm her boyfriend and haven't seen her since her car accident.

I cringe, but I use it.

We need to talk.

As soon as she puts her hand on my thigh under the table at Perks and Rec, I push my chair back and say, with a sweet smile, "Can I talk to you for a minute? Alone?"

Violet seems to think that's a great idea and readily agrees. She leads me over to an area of the café that is all bookcases and armchairs gathered around coffee tables.

There are still too many people, though.

"How about outside?" I ask.

"Sure." She slips her hand in mine, and I let her lead me out the front door.

I don't look around to see where Thea is or if she's watching. It's been hard enough watching her wait tables, acting as if she barely knows me. We haven't made eye contact or spoken direct words to one another since we left the football field.

I don't know what she said to her friends, but I have been getting death glares from Andi. The looks from Nora are more sympathetic, which maybe makes me even more nervous.

"Sorry, I need these," Violet says, slipping her sunglasses on as we stop on the sidewalk.

"Of course." I'm aware that we are right in front of the window of Perks and Rec, and everyone inside can see us. But at least they can't hear us. "I am really glad to see you and that you're doing well," I start.

She steps forward and takes my hand again. "Thank you. I can't believe you're the one who saved me. That's amazing."

I don't pull my hand away, knowing those optics would be terrible. "I'm glad I was on that same road. But there's something I have to tell you."

"Okay."

"I have had a great time with Merry Mayhem, and I love your family and your town."

Her smile is wide and bright. "I'm so glad. They love you, too. They can't quit talking about you. When Harley told me that you're the one who was there when he had his stroke and that he's been in touch with you all these months, I just knew this was meant to be."

I shake my head. "That's the thing." I take a breath. "I can't date you for real. There's someone else."

I see her brows lift over the top of the sunglasses. "Oh."

"I'm sorry. The night we decided to do this, it was really about Sam, and you not wanting to face him alone. We didn't really talk about what would happen after Merry Mayhem."

She slips her hand out of mine and tucks both hands in the front pocket of the hoodie she is wearing. "You're right. We didn't. I was so focused on the fact that Chad was ditching me, and that this was coming up, that I just wanted to get through the weekend."

"Yeah, and then when you had your accident, I didn't want to make any decisions about what I told people or did without you," I say honestly.

"That's really decent of you," she says. "What does your girlfriend think about all of this, though? You helping me out by pretending to be my boyfriend?"

"That's…actually a new development," I say. That's not entirely untrue.

"So things changed between you just since I've been in the hospital? But you couldn't do anything about it because you couldn't talk to me about it, and you'd already promised to do this with me."

"Pretty much."

She laughs lightly and shakes her head. "You're a really good guy, Josh. I don't know many guys who would do that."

"Well, I've told her the full truth about the agreement between you and me. And that we barely knew each other. That there aren't any feelings here."

"I see." She frowns. "And she's agreed to keep that to herself?"

"Yeah, for sure. She understood."

"Wow, she must be great. And totally trust you. And be totally sure of your feelings."

"She *is* amazing," I say. "And I hope she's sure of my feelings. I will say, she's a little concerned now, though, about how you and I end this without it still looking bad in front of Sam."

Violet sighs and shrugs. "You and I just say we broke up. I mean, seeing Sam here with Ashley actually makes me realize that we just weren't meant to be. And I'm glad we didn't do something stupid like get married just because we've been together for a long time. Or just assumed that that was as good as it was ever going to be."

I study her. That's actually a great attitude. "You're not bothered that he's here at all?"

She laughs. "I wouldn't say that. And I think it's weird that he and Ashley are engaged already. But being in a car accident and a coma for a couple of days has a way of putting things into perspective. There are way more important things in my life than my ex-boyfriend and his new fiancée."

"I have to say, I'm still really glad that Chad ended up being a jerk and I was able to step in for Merry Mayhem. I've had a great time."

"Everyone says you have fit right in." She studies me for a moment. "Does this girlfriend know how great you are?"

I cannot tell her that it's Thea. These two women have a relationship, and it is up to Thea to tell Violet how she feels and what she wants. I have to follow Muriel's advice here and let Thea take the lead on this.

But I nod. "I actually think she has very strong feelings for me. I just think she's…scared."

"Scared of what?"

I've thought about this, and I think I know the answer. Because I've felt the same way about the people who are important to me.

"She made some mistakes, and the people she loves were there for her and supported her. But she felt she had to make up for that. So, she's spent a very long time being dependable, predictable, and taking care of others. She's always the person everyone thinks she is and expects her to be. I think she's scared of doing something that will surprise them and might disappoint a few people."

Violet smiles. "Well, I hope she takes that chance."

"Yeah?" I hope Violet feels that way when she finds out that she's one of the people Thea doesn't want to disappoint.

"For sure. I know personally how great it is to mess up and have the people you love be there for you anyway. So I hope she gets to find that out."

I really like all of Thea's family, it turns out. "I really hope she takes that chance too," I say.

"And I can't imagine how anyone would think being with *you* is some kind of mess-up."

And I really hope that Violet's memory is, in fact, fully intact so that she remembers saying that when everything comes out.

❄

THE TENSION between Thea and me—and her stubborn determination not to look at or talk to me—is not a problem during the afternoon Merry Mayhan challenge.

The scavenger hunt takes us all around town, but the pairs are, obviously, split up.

Muriel and I come in third after Thea and Patty in first, and Beckett and Sutton in second place.

This leaves us with the issue of living in the same house and just across the hall from one another. The hallway where I stripped her naked and made her come before taking her into her bedroom and fucking her all night long.

Unfortunately, Thea doesn't want to relive those memories. Apparently, even in her head.

She's even avoiding her own house.

When I show up at her house after the scavenger hunt, Bruce and Bebe are there.

"I'm sorry, sweetheart," Bebe says. "But I took it upon myself to pack your things. Violet wasn't feeling well and needed to lie down."

Of course she did. She's suffering from a major concussion.

And I was sleeping in her room.

"Of course it's fine," I tell Bebe.

I'm grateful that I didn't need to dig out the condoms the night before, now for a reason even beyond how amazing it was to fuck Thea without one. God knows, in my haste to get back to her bedroom, I would have just upended my toiletry bag in the middle of the room.

"I don't mean to insinuate that you can't stay here with Violet," Bebe says quickly. "I just moved your things so that she could lie down."

I shake my head. God, I can't stay here in Violet's room with her. "No, of course. She needs time and space to rest. I was thinking maybe I should drive back to Autre."

Bebe's eyes go wide. "But there's still a lot of Merry Mayhem left. No, you can stay over at Bruce and Harley's. They have an extra room."

I'm relieved. The drive to and from Autre is too far in case there's a surprise challenge, but more, I want to be close in case Thea wants to talk.

This isn't over between us. I'm not exactly sure how we're going to fix this whole thing, but Violet and I are okay. Maybe once Violet tells her sister that, and about our conversation, Thea will come clean with Violet.

"That would be great if it's not an inconvenience," I say.

Bruce overhears. "Don't be silly. We're having people over tonight to play cards. You're welcome to join. Or to just hang out with us."

I'm actually praying for a surprise challenge, but anything to take my mind off the fact that I'm madly in love and can't do a damn thing about it is welcome.

A few hours later, I am sitting on Bruce and Harley's couch, nursing a very strong mix of something that's supposed to be an apple cinnamon cocktail but is absolutely mostly whiskey.

Not that I'm complaining.

Bruce and Harley are playing cards with Brewser, Wilson, and Leo and Ellie Landry.

I feel perfectly comfortable around all of them, even after just a couple of days. I've always loved being with Leo and Ellie, and spending time with this group feels like being with them. They are no bullshit, warm, welcoming, fully accepting people. I love them.

But I can't concentrate on a card game, so I brought myself over to the couch where I'm watching a Sandra Bullock Christmas movie.

The irony that the man she thinks she's in love with is in a coma while she's falling in love with his brother is not lost on me.

But I don't change the channel.

I'm still keeping my phone close and alternately hoping for a surprise challenge or a text from Thea, but it's nearly ten now and I'm starting to lose hope.

Ellie Landry sinks onto the couch next to me after they finish another hand of cards, and everyone takes a break to refill drinks and snacks.

"You've had a fun few days here in Rebel, sounds like," she says, her eyes on the screen.

"I have."

"They all love you. I knew they would."

I nod and sip, swallow, then say, "I love them too."

"I knew you would," she says.

We are past the part of the movie where Sandra Bullock's character has confessed to the family friend that she and the guy in the coma were never actually engaged or even involved.

Ellie is the only one in this room who knows my truth.

"How mad are they gonna be if I'm not in love with Violet?" I ask her softly.

"Violet's a great girl."

"I know. But she's not the right girl. She's not the one."

"You're sure? She just got home."

"It's not about her so much as it is about already finding the girl. The one. Someone else."

Ellie reaches out and takes my glass from my fingers, takes a long drink of my cocktail, and hands it back. She doesn't even grimace.

"Have you told Violet that you're in love with Thea?"

It's not just the whiskey that makes me react with absolutely no surprise to Ellie Landry knowing exactly who I'm talking about. Ellie always knows everything.

"No. I thought that was probably Thea's thing to tell her. I did tell her there was someone else, though."

Ellie laughs. "Oh wow, I give her about five minutes tomorrow to figure it out. She's a smart girl."

"For Violet to figure it out?"

"Honey, you're a wonderful firefighter and paramedic, you're funny, you don't have a bad singing voice, and you're a pretty decent shot on the basketball court from what I've seen, but you're a terrible actor. If you feel about Thea the way you feel about the other people in your life, you're not gonna be able to hide it even if you try."

Ellie has known me for about two years. She is surrounded by people who live life loud and fully. They love hard. I consider everything she just said about me to be a compliment.

"I don't wanna cause problems for anybody," I say.

"And why not?"

I snort. "Because being a problem for people is generally a bad thing." I should know.

"When you started going to the support group for gambling, were your friends and family happy for you?"

I confessed about my past to Ellie and Leo a long time ago. "Very."

"And when you got your gambling debts all paid off, did they hug you and tell you they were proud of you?"

"Yes." Leo and Ellie had also hugged me and told me they were proud of me.

"And when you went a year, and then two, without gambling, were they excited for you?"

"Definitely."

"And when you got through the fire academy, were they happy and did they celebrate for you?"

"They did."

"So even though you were a "problem"," she says, making air quotes, "They still cheered for you and supported you and loved you, right?"

"Of course."

"So you know, firsthand, that you can make mistakes and still be loved."

I nod, my throat tight.

"Be a person who lives your life in such a way that when you find love and joy, the people around you are thrilled for you.

You're doing that, Josh. And I can promise you that Thea Chabert lives that life. You two being crazy about each other might surprise people for a minute, but they'll be happy for you both. Trust that you deserve this and that good people will believe that. And fuck the people who don't."

I sigh. But it's definitely with some relief. What she says makes sense. If people care about Thea and me, they will want us to be happy. And I do believe that these people sitting at the table behind me, and honestly, this entire town, love Thea a lot. Anyone who doesn't is an idiot.

"So it sounds to me like you're saying I need a grand gesture for Thea," I say.

Ellie's eyes practically sparkle at those words. The Landry family loves nothing more than a grand love gesture.

"What I know is that you are going to be somewhere tomorrow where the entire town is gonna show up, there's going to be a microphone, and a confetti canon."

I laugh and feel a huge weight lift from my chest. She has a point. It's not every day a guy is given a chance to confess his life with a confetti canon.

"Love you, Ellie."

She gives me a wink. "How could you not?" Then she gets up from the couch, leans over, and kisses me on top of the head and says, "And now I know where I'm gonna be tomorrow."

CHAPTER 19
THEA

"YOU DON'T LOOK sick to me," I tell Patty.

She and Muriel are sitting in the front row, right by the ice.

Patty has on a gorgeous white fake fur coat and is sipping from a bedazzled red thermos. It smells like peppermint schnapps with a little hot cocoa added.

She gives a light, very fake cough. "It's just a tickle." She takes a dainty sip. "But I don't want to do anything to make it worse."

I look from her to Muriel, who is also in fake fur. Hers is Cookie Monster blue. She's also wearing a yellow bucket hat with a large purple bow.

"You both have a tickle in your throat?"

Muriel coughs hard. "Must be going around," she says. "You'll have to team up with Josh again. We can't possibly play today."

Andi and I had spent this morning trying to figure out a way to put skis on the ladies' grocery carts so they could be out on the ice of the hockey rink with us for Peppermint Puck-A-Palooza.

But we couldn't find the carts. Muriel and Patty have stashed them somewhere.

And then we'd been informed the Coffelt twins were pulling out of today's events.

They'd also suggested that Josh and I team up again, and Nora had assured me that she and the judges were fine with that.

Uh, huh.

Nora knows about me and Josh.

I think Patty and Muriel suspect.

They're playing matchmaker and…

I wish it were that easy.

"Come on, Hot Wheels, let's get you in your cart." Josh skates up next to me, addressing Muriel with a grin.

Muriel shakes her head and sips from her own sparkly hot pink thermos. "Can't do it, I'm very sick."

Josh lifts a skeptical brow and glances at me. I roll my eyes.

"You're scared of playing a little hockey with plastic candy canes?" he asks Muriel. "What if I tell you that I played hockey in a rec league all through high school and college?" he asks.

Muriel perks up. "Did you now?"

"We have snow and ice in Nebraska," he says. "Makes more sense for me to play hockey than all these boys down here in Louisiana."

Muriel cackles. "It does, doesn't it? And yet here we are in a little town on the bayou with an ice-skating rink and a hockey team."

I look down at Josh's feet. "Where did you even get skates?"

He lifts a foot. "Beckett."

Of course. Makes sense that the guy who actually plays hockey and gets paid for it might have an extra pair or two lying around.

"That was nice of him," I comment.

"See?" Muriel says. "I am leaving you with a very capable partner."

Patty elbows her, and Muriel coughs.

It is possibly the fakest cough I've ever heard in my life.

Josh looks at me. "We're partners again, huh?"

Even standing this close to him is hard on my heart rate. I had prepared myself for seeing him today, probably even talking to him at some point. But I'm not sure I can be his partner.

I look back at the two older ladies who are very settled into their seats in their cozy coats, sipping hot chocolate.

But I don't really have a choice.

"I guess," I say.

He gives Patty and Muriel a wink and says to me, "Then it's just you and me."

I narrow my eyes. "Did you plan this with them?"

He turns to face me. "I have no idea what you mean."

I look at the two older women who are volunteering nothing. "Did you ask them to sit this out so we had to be partners?"

"I didn't. But I'm not going to say I'm upset about it." He looks at Muriel and Patty. "No offense."

"If you were upset about being her partner today, you'd be a dumbass. And you're not a dumbass," Muriel says, taking another swig of cocoa.

He shrugs and looks at me. "You can't argue with that logic."

Jingle bells ring out, and Nora's voice comes over the mic. "We have a last-minute change, everyone. Muriel and Patty are feeling under the weather, so Josh and Thea will be partnering up again. We'll...figure out the points somehow, later. Josh and Thea, we need you at center ice with Max and Mitchell."

I find Nora across the ice from us.

She's decked out in an oversized hockey jersey from the local team, the Rebel Rebels—of course—paired with leggings, a sparkly Christmas garland around her neck with a gigantic whistle attached, and a headband with reindeer antlers on her head.

I shake my head.

Someday, Nora is going to dress the way Muriel does now. I just know it.

Maybe I can be the Patty to her Muriel. I slide a look at the older women again. There is something very appealing about just doing whatever the fuck I want to. In faux fur and sparkles.

"You ready?" Josh asks.

Fine, I can do this. This event is very fast-paced, and it's not like we're going to have time to talk. We are literally on the ice, being watched by everyone. We have fifteen minutes, so we can't mess around—not like that stopped us yesterday during the obstacle course, but today we're going to *focus*.

We're going to get this event done, then we'll build a stupid gingerbread house, and then we're done.

Merry Mayhem will be over.

Josh will go back to Autre.

And I will start working on getting over him.

Sure. That seems simple enough.

"Sure."

We skate to center ice and join Max and Mitchell. They grin with excitement.

"Mitchell, you guys will be green, Josh and Thea, you're red," Nora instructs.

This event is more or less like billiards on ice.

Kind of.

Peppermint Puck-A-Palooza is basically a game that Nora made up. Of course. Nora is the mastermind behind everything Parks and Rec does, but when it comes to hockey, she's even more over-the-top. She might've had some help from Andi or Everly, maybe even Beckett, but Puck-A-Palooza is basically what would happen if hockey and billiards got together and had a baby. And the baby had hockey pucks ten times the usual size, and there were seven pucks for each team—so fourteen pucks on the ice at once—plus two white pucks that we're supposed to use to hit the pucks into the nets.

Oh, and we're using giant plastic candy canes instead of hockey sticks.

But sure, it's just like hockey. And billiards.

"Get ready, get set, go!" Nora shouts.

There's no confetti canon for this event since the confetti

would make skating over the ice very difficult, and I can tell that bothers Nora a little bit. She really likes her confetti canon.

There's also no puck drop like in hockey. We just all skate off and start trying to hit a white puck into our colored pucks.

Beckett and Sutton played earlier, along with Sam and Ashley. Beckett scored more points than anyone ever has for this event, as should be expected of a semi-pro hockey player, I suppose.

The team here in Rebel is only an FPHL league team, so minor *minor* league. Still, he gets a paycheck for playing hockey, so that puts him ahead of anyone who does it just for fun. A little anyway.

Truthfully, our team sucks, and they're having trouble putting butts in the seats. If our resident billionaire—my cousin, Dane—didn't own the hockey rink and keep it running, the rink would've been shut down a long time ago, and the team would be long gone.

I let Josh take the first couple of shots, and he does get a puck into the net, but I'm no slouch on the ice. Sure, it might be unusual for a Louisiana girl to know how to ice skate, but we've had the ice rink here for a few years, and Ruth wanted to take lessons, so I did it with her. I can skate, and I actually love hockey, so I skate after the white puck that Josh just sent sailing. I send one of our red pucks into a side net, and Josh skates over to give me a high five.

"Good job," he says with a grin.

"Thanks. You, too." I glance behind him. "Max and Mitchell both play youth hockey, by the way."

Josh grimaces. "Dammit."

I laugh. "Technically, we're still competing against all of the other teams. It's all about how many times we can put the puck in the net in fifteen minutes. Just focus on that."

"It's actually really hard to focus on anything. I want to kiss you so badly."

My eyes widen. "Josh, stop it."

"Nobody can hear what I'm saying out here."

"Still, you can't say stuff like that. It's way too hard for me not to react, and we can't do anything about it anyway."

"I talked to Violet. Did you two talk?"

No, we didn't. On purpose. "Can we discuss this after?"

"Will you discuss it with me after? Or will you disappear?"

That's a fair question. I actually planned to disappear. Spending time with him, in close proximity, is way too hard.

"Fine, we can talk after."

"I'm going to hold you to that. Otherwise, I might have to make a scene," he says with a little half smile.

"You're threatening me?"

"Is hearing that I'm falling in love with you and am determined to find a way to make this work a threat, Danger?"

His voice is low and gruff now, and the look in his eyes is one that I would very much like to see for the rest of my life.

I take a deep breath. It's shaky, and I feel like it doesn't actually give me the boost of oxygen or clarity that I need. "I don't know what to do."

"Trust that your sister loves you. Tell her the truth."

"You didn't tell her everything?" I ask. But I already know the answer. He wouldn't do that to me.

"I told her that nothing could happen between her and me. Because there's someone else. But I'd really like it if you'd claim me."

His words hit me directly in the heart.

He spent two years hung up on a woman who never would claim him. A woman he changed his entire life around for. I know now that he's happy about those changes, even if things didn't work out with her, but she didn't want him, even when he gave her everything.

He's letting me take the lead here with my sister, and I appreciate that, but I know what it would mean to him if I took a risk for him.

"Are you guys okay?" Max and Mitchell have skated up to us, concerned looks on their faces.

I'm not sure I am okay, but I nod. "Yeah, we're fine."

"Are you sure? You've scored like two goals in ten minutes."

My eyes fly to the clock, and sure enough, we only have five minutes left. "Crap." I look at Josh. "I heard you. We'll figure it out."

He nods. "Okay."

"But right now? We need to go try to score some points."

"Let's go, *partner*."

Yeah, yeah, I get his meaning. And I want that too.

We skate quickly to where the white puck is resting, and I shoot it over to him. He uses it to hit one of the red pucks into the closest net.

I go after it, fishing it out of the net and shooting it to him again. He sends the white puck sliding into another red one, but it goes careening far left of the net. I skate after it, assuming he'll position himself in front of the net so that I can shoot it out to him. I glance to where I expect him to be, but he's not, which pulls my attention even further to the right. My skate catches against the edge of the net, and suddenly I'm falling.

I'm more surprised than anything and I whip my arm out, trying to grab onto the net to keep myself up.

The net simply tips over with me.

I hit the ice hard on my right hip, and the net crashes down on top of me, whacking me in the head.

"Thea!" I hear Josh yell.

"Holy shit!" one of the twins shouts.

I just lay still for a second with my eyes squeezed shut. My head hurts, but my hip hurts worse. And then of course there's my ego. A bunch of people just saw that happen.

Suddenly, the net shifts off of me, and I take a deep breath.

I feel Josh kneeling next to me. He slides one big hand under my head, cradling it gently. "Thea, sweetheart, are you okay?"

"Did she get knocked out?" one of the twins asks.

"Did she break anything?" the other asks.

I open my eyes to show the boys that I'm alive.

"I'm in one piece," I tell them.

"Wow, that was…" one of them starts.

"Not graceful," the other fills in.

I laugh and close my eyes again because that makes my head twinge.

"Thea, keep your eyes open for me," Josh urges.

"No," I say. Mostly because I really like his hand on my head and him leaning over me like this. He smells really good and his body is warm.

"Danger, come on now, open your eyes," he coaxes. "Let me see those pretty blues."

I moan because I love that nickname and how his voice sounds right now. Turns out his reassuring, paramedic sweet-talk sounds a little like his bedroom sweet-talk. I open my eyes for him.

He's leaning over me, and our gazes lock.

God, I love his eyes. And his mouth.

All of him. I love all of him.

I really don't want to give up looking into his eyes. Or his mouth. I don't want to give up the right to be this close to him, to have his hands on me, to hear this low, rough voice.

"There you go. Are you hurt?"

"Yes. Ice is very hard."

He huffs out a laugh. "Yes, it is. Which is why you shouldn't fall down on it."

"I'll try to remember that," I say, letting my eyes slide shut again.

"Hey," he says, rubbing his hand over the back of my head. "We can't have two Chabert girls with concussions."

"It's not a concussion. I'm okay. But if I open my eyes, you might stop."

"Stop what?" he asks. I can hear the amusement in his tone, though he still sounds concerned.

"Touching me and being sexy Mr. paramedic," I say.

He's quiet for a second, then he says, "I think I'll keep being a paramedic for a little bit if that's okay with you. I wanna be sure you're all right. Can we get you up off the ice?"

"If you keep your hands on me. And if we can role-play paramedic and patient later."

He gives a cough-choke sound. I open my eyes and look up at him. And realize there are about a dozen people gathered around us.

Oh. Crap.

"Oops," I say, meeting his gaze again.

"And to think, I was going to use a confetti canon to tell everyone how I feel about you."

I'm not sure what to say to that, and I'm saved from having to reply by Josh, Max, and Mitchell lifting me and helping me to skate over to one of the benches the hockey teams occupy during games. We sit, and Brewser comes over. Between the retired doctor and the current paramedic, they decide I'm going to be fine. Someone hands me an ice pack, someone else hands me two ibuprofen and a bottle of water, and Nora wants to know if she can go ahead with the final team for Peppermint Puck-A-Palooza.

I am very happy just to sit on the bench next to Josh and watch Jesse and Brad knock their pucks around the ice for fifteen minutes.

We don't talk, but Josh does link his pinky with mine on the bench between our thighs.

And I know, then and there, that I need to talk to my sister as soon as possible.

"Are you sure you feel okay?" Josh asks as we skate over to exit the ice fifteen minutes later.

I look up at him. "My head and my hip are fine. But my heart is a little achy."

His eyes flare with emotion, and his lips part as if he's about to respond.

But just then I hear, "It's *Thea*?"

We turn to find Violet blocking our exit.

Her hands are on her hips, and she's looking at us with an expectant expression.

"Hi. I was just going to come find you," I say.

"I've been here the whole time," she says, looking from me to Josh and then back. "I saw you two down on the ice." She looks at Josh. "Why didn't you tell me that you're in love with my *sister*?"

I suck in a little breath and feel Josh stiffen next to me.

Violet rolls her eyes. "Really? Everyone here could tell. I mean, I know you're a great paramedic and all, but I'm guessing you didn't look at me like that when you were pulling me out of the car."

"Pulling you out of a car in a ditch is a whole different situation than checking Thea out on the ice after she fell," Josh says.

Violet laughs. "Yes. And you have your heart in your throat because the woman you're in love with fell over and bumped her head. It looks a whole lot different than you, being a professional and helping a patient out of a car accident."

He opens his mouth to respond again, then shuts it and turns to look at me. "I guess we could just tell her now."

I look at my sister. "We didn't mean for this to happen."

She steps forward and takes my face in her hands. "Why didn't you tell me?"

"That I *stole* your *boyfriend* while you were in a *coma*?" I ask her. I reach up and grip her wrists. "Because what the hell kind of sister am I?"

She shakes her head. "God, Thea. Josh and I just met. You weren't stealing anything."

"But..."

"But you have always taken care of me, so you couldn't think of yourself for even a second," she fills in when I trail off. She gives me a soft smile. "You take care of everyone. It's probably why you and Josh clicked so quickly. You're both caretakers."

That hits me harder than I think Violet even intended. She's right.

Josh and I have also both made big mistakes in the past that affected the people we love, and we both feel a constant urge to make up for those. But that doesn't change the fact that we love taking care of people and are really fucking good at it.

"That's one of the things I love most about him," I admit.

"I wish you had told me," Violet says, almost sadly.

I take her hands from my face, but link our fingers. "I knew how important it was for you to have him while you were facing Sam. I don't want this to be hard on you with Sam here."

She rolls her eyes. "You being happy is so much more important to me than looking good in front of Sam. Sure, Sam hurt me and broke my heart. I will get over that. You and Josh not being together is not something either of you will get over. You being in love and loved by a guy like Josh?" She looks up at him and smiles. "This is exactly what I want for you, Thea. You deserve this."

Tears prick at the back of my eyes. "You're really okay, even with Sam here?"

"I'm better than okay. In fact, I've decided that facing Sam as a happy, independent, confident single woman is even better than facing him with a new boyfriend."

I squeeze her hands. "You *are* a strong, independent, confident woman."

She nods. "Yeah, it was just the happy part I wasn't sure about. But I am that. My car accident really showed me that I have so much to be grateful for and happy about. And now I can be happy about my big sister falling in love with an amazing guy."

The tears finally slip over my lower lashes, and I lean in, pulling Violet close. She wraps her arms around me, and I squeeze her tightly.

"Thank you," I say.

"For what?" she asks. "I'd be a real asshole to stand in the way of you and Josh."

"Just for being an awesome sister."

"Yeah, well, I learned from the best."

CHAPTER 20
JOSH

THEA and I climb onto the stage in the middle of Main Street for the final challenge of Merry Mayhem.

We head for the third long table, which is our station for the Great Gingerbread Dash. We will be racing the other teams to see who can use every single item on the table in front of us to build the best-looking gingerbread house in ten minutes or less. The first group to finish something that looks decent gets one hundred points, the second group gets fifty, and the third group gets ten. Everyone else gets nothing.

Even if we get a hundred points, Thea and I are not winning this thing.

And neither of us cares.

"I really want to grab that microphone and announce to this entire town that I'm madly in love with you," I say conversationally.

Thea trips over her feet, and I grab her elbow with a grin.

"Tell me you're not going to do that," she says, as we move behind the table.

"No promises," I say.

I want to do something. Not just because Ellie Landry is in the front row for the event and I kind of want the Landry family grand gesture stamp of approval—though, I do—but because my feelings for Thea feel big and bright and like they might just explode out of me at any moment. Like a confetti canon.

And because I want everyone to know about us.

I came to Rebel, Louisiana, and signed up for Merry Mayhem to take my mind off being alone and wasting two years of my life chasing the idea of love instead of the real thing.

But I got swept up in the fun and joy and these people.

And this person beside me.

I don't want this to end.

While I know Merry Mayhem is over today, I feel that everything that makes it so fun, joyful, and yes, a little bonkers, is really everyday life here in Rebel. I want more of these people, their love for one another, their love for life, the way they celebrate things, and support each other.

And Thea. God, I want more of her. All of her. Instead of letting that end today, I want this to be the start.

"Josh, we still have to let Violet figure out how she wants to handle the whole 'my boyfriend is now with my sister' thing," Thea says quietly. "If you just make some big announcement, you still put a spotlight on her that she might not want."

"That's the only reason I'm not kissing you right now up on this stage in the middle of town," I tell her, checking out the gingerbread house pieces and parts in front of us as if we're discussing whether white or multi-colored lights are better on a tree.

Because it is like that. It's going to be a normal daily occurrence for me to let Thea Chabert know that I love and want her. She'll get used to it.

Or she'll catch her breath and freeze for a second, and her eyes will go wide every single time for the next seventy-five years of her life, like she did just now.

Either way, I'm going to do it.

I look away from the multitudes of candy and bowls of thick frosting to find her staring at me.

"Do you hate the idea of me kissing you in public? Because we're going to need to discuss that. Once it's okay to do, I'm going to want to. A lot."

She shakes her head. "That's not what I was thinking about."

Her cheeks are a little pink. I grin and lean in, even though I'm supposed to behave. "What were you thinking about?"

"All the places I'd like you to kiss me. And my mouth is like number three on the list at the moment if I'm honest."

Now I'm the one who catches his breath and freezes.

"This is why I call you Danger," I say in a low growl.

She opens her mouth—I'm sure to remind me of where we are —when the jingle bells start ringing, indicating the start of the next challenge.

I straighten, but say, "Raincheck."

She is clearly fighting a smile.

Nora takes the microphone. "Hi, everyone!"

The crowd cheers.

"It's our last event!" she says.

The crowd boos.

Nora laughs. "I know, I know. But Santa comes tonight, so we need to get cleaned up and ready for him!"

More cheering.

"And don't forget, we have lots of fun planned for Valentine's Day!"

More cheering.

I look down at Thea. "Valentine's Day?"

"Oh, of course, there's all kinds of stuff going on for Valentine's Day," she says.

I'm going to need to hear more about this.

"But, before we get to the Gingerbread Dash," Nora goes on. "There is one thing I want to do. The Merry Mayhem board of directors has the name of this year's Peppermint Princess!"

The entire crowd is quiet. Everyone turns to look at the person next to them. Then there's soft murmuring.

"Since when do we have a Peppermint Princess?" someone yells.

Nora nods. "Since right now."

"We just added it?" someone else asks.

Nora shrugs. "Yep! It's not like we have a *rule* that says we can't."

People start nodding, and there's a smattering of laughter that ripples through the crowd.

"Why do I get the feeling that Nora really likes this no rules thing?" I ask Thea.

"Yeah, she's really getting into that," Thea agrees. "I guess it makes her job with all the events and clubs that Parks and Rec organizes easier if there are fewer rules."

I laugh. "That might come back and bite her in the ass."

"Well? Who is it?" someone calls out.

"This year's Peppermint Princess is Violet Chabert!" Nora says happily.

Everyone cheers and starts applauding.

The crowd parts as Violet makes her way toward the stage.

Nora produces a crown made of candy canes, which I assume are plastic, and a red cape with white fur trim. She places the crown on Violet's head while Harley drapes the cape around Violet's shoulders.

"And no one even blinks that the winner is the Mayor's granddaughter and the organizer's cousin?" I ask Thea.

She laughs. "Oh, lord, no."

Nora hands Violet the microphone, and Violet takes it with a big grin.

"Well, thank you." She faces the crowd. "When I asked Nora if I could say a few words, this is not at all what I expected."

The crowd cheers.

"I wanted a chance to say thank you," Violet says, quieting the noise. "I can't believe the amount of support and love I've felt over these past few days after my accident, and I wanted to say how much I love all of you. I've always felt like Rebel is one big family, and you've all just driven that point home to me. Thank you." She sniffs, and everyone applauds again.

"And there's something I need to tell you," she continues. "Something that you've all given me the strength to say."

She glances toward me and Thea, and I feel my spine tense.

Oh. She's going to do this right now.

"Oh…crap," Thea says.

"It's good," I tell her. "Let her do it."

"She doesn't have to do it like *this*."

"She has to do it however she wants to," I say quietly.

"Josh is not my boyfriend," Violet says. Not quietly.

Just like that. Clear and simple.

"He's a great guy who agreed to help me out when I needed a friend."

She looks at me again and gives me a smile. That I return. But I'm itching to take Thea's hand.

"I thought that I couldn't face Merry Mayhem and this holiday without Sam. Single. Alone," she goes on, facing the crowd again. "So, I asked Josh a *huge* favor—to pretend to be my boyfriend for a few days—and he said yes. But it isn't true. Josh and I were never together. We met at Perks and Rec the night of my accident. Then he pulled me out of the car and got me to the hospital. He saved me, physically, but…" She pauses and takes a deep breath. "*You* all saved my heart. You showed me over these past two days how loved I am. How much support I have. That I'm absolutely not alone at all. I will never be alone. I might not have a boyfriend, but I'm very loved and I don't want to be anywhere, with anyone other than all of you for Christmas."

She stops, and the entire crowd is quiet for several long seconds.

Then someone starts clapping. Quickly, more join in, and soon everyone is clapping and cheering. Several people are wiping their eyes, but everyone is smiling.

Violet stands smiling out at the town.

"Wow," Thea says quietly.

"That was really good," I say.

"Yeah. I'm so proud of her."

Then Violet turns to us. "And *now,* Josh, you can kiss my sister the way I know you're dying to."

Surprise rocks through me, but I'm not an idiot. I turn to Thea, cup her face, and kiss her before she can think of a reason why I shouldn't.

The applause and cheering gets even louder.

And Thea kisses me back.

She slides her hand to the back of my neck as I tip her back and lets me *really* kiss her.

The next thing I know, I hear the *boom* of the confetti canon, and red, green, and white sparkly paper is raining down around us.

I pull back and grin down at Thea. "Well, there was still a stage, a mic, and confetti, even if I wasn't the one making the big public speech."

She laughs. "Sorry, your grand gesture was just a kiss."

I shake my head. "As long as everyone knows you're mine."

She sighs happily. "Too bad we still need to build our gingerbread house."

"I'm willing to forfeit and keep making out with you instead."

She presses her lips together, and her cheeks get pink.

"What are you thinking?" I ask, *needing* to know.

"Just about all the places I'd like to smear frosting and stick candy. And I'm not talking about gingerbread."

That's it. The mayhem this woman is going to cause in my life isn't over, but we're moving locations for now.

I bend, haul her over my shoulder, stand, grab a bag of candy and a bowl of frosting, and head for the stage steps.

She's laughing and wiggling, though not enough to actually get away. "Josh! We'll lose!"

I grin and wave to the crowd that's laughing and cheering for us.

"Oh, Danger, we already won this whole damned thing."

. . .

Thank you so much for reading Merry Mayhem!
I hope you loved Josh and Thea's story!

There's so much more to come from Rebel, Louisiana!
Nora's book is next!

Find all my books at
www.ErinNicholas.com
including a printable book list
on the top of the "books" page!

And join in on all the FAN FUN!

And the best place to find out all the news about that (including title and cover reveal, release date, and more!) is right here:
bit.ly/Keep-In-Touch-Erin
(be sure you get those capital letters and dashes in there!)

And this is your personal invitation to my Facebook group, **Erin Nicholas's Super Fans** where you can get first looks, behind the scenes peeks, and daily fun with fellow romance lovers (including me!)!

IF YOU LOVE REBEL, LOUISIANA

You're going to love Autre just as much!

Check out the Boys of the Bayou and the Boys of the Bayou Gone Wild!
All available now!

Boys of the Bayou

My Best Friend's Mardi Gras Wedding (Josh & Tori)

Sweet Home Louisiana (Owen & Maddie)

Beauty and the Bayou (Sawyer & Juliet)

Crazy Rich Cajuns (Bennett & Kennedy)

Must Love Alligators (Chase & Bailey)

Four Weddings and a Swamp Boat Tour (Mitch & Paige)

Boys of the Bayou Gone Wild

Otterly Irresistible (Charlie& Griffin)

Heavy Petting (Fletcher & Jordan)

Flipping Love You (Zeke & Jill)

Sealed With a Kiss (Donovan & Naomi)

Head Over Hooves (Drew & Rory)

Say It Like You Mane It (Zander & Caroline)

Kiss My Giraffe (Knox & Fiona)

Better Safe Than Safari (Colin & Hayden)

And much more—

including my printable booklist— at

ErinNicholas.com

ABOUT ERIN

Erin Nicholas is the New York Times and USA Today bestselling author of over sixty sexy contemporary romances. She's known for her blue-collar book boyfriends and big, boisterous found families in small towns. Her stories have been described as toe-curling, enchanting, steamy and fun.

She lives in the Midwest with her husband who only wants to read the sex scenes in her books, her kids who will never read the sex scenes in her books, and family and friends who say they're shocked by the sex scenes in her books (yeah, right!).

Find her and all her books at
www.ErinNicholas.com

And find her on Facebook, BookBub, Goodreads, and Instagram!

Editor: Becky Burrier, Bookcase Media

Cover design: Qamber Designs

Digital ISBN: 978-1-967534-11-1

Paperback ISBN: 978-1-967534-12-8

9 781967 534128